Edge of DESIRE

JESSICA MARIN

Edge of DESIRE

Prologue

Cora

The Past

THERE HAVEN'T BEEN many things in my life that have scared me.

My mother taking us away from my drunk of a father when I was four didn't scare me.

Moving every few years after my mother got dumped by her ex-boyfriends didn't scare me.

Having to start new schools every time we moved didn't scare me.

Every time my mother slapped me across my face didn't scare me.

But staring up at the ominous, gothic looking building that's supposed to be my new boarding school … scares me.

"Mother, why do I have to go away to school?" I whine, not understanding what I've done this time for her to banish me from our home. I was behaving at my former school, despite the hatred and jealousy that oozes from the other girls there. Jealousy over my looks, which in turn, makes them hate me when all the boys want me instead of them. I can't help that I was born beautiful. I can't help the attention I receive from men. Those bitches should want to be my friend so they can have a shot at my leftovers. I was finally settling into a nice routine when my mother dropped the bomb that I will now be going to boarding school.

"Stop whining, Cora. You've been given an opportunity to attend one of the most prestigious boarding schools in the UK, so be a little bit more grateful," she retorts while tugging my hand harder in order for me to keep up with her pace.

The "opportunity" being given to me by her current boyfriend, who is extremely wealthy. Despite him being half her age, overweight and ugly, she still spreads her legs for him in order to have the lifestyle she believes she deserves.

"But I don't want to go away!" I pull my hand free from hers and stop walking. I cross my arms over my chest, stomp my foot, and glare at her. If I put up more of a fight, maybe she will forget where we are and hit me in front of witnesses—preferably the headmaster—who will then banish us from the school. I learned from a young age that being naughty was the only time I received any attention from my mother.

She turns around and approaches me, her steel gray eyes turning hard, her hands fisting at her sides. I bite my lip to keep the smug smile of satisfaction from appearing on my face since I know what that look of hers means. I brace myself for the impact of her hand across my face, but to my surprise, she grips my arms instead and squeezes, not caring when I yelp out in pain.

"Listen closely, you little brat." She leans in closer, whispering harshly into my ear. "You will keep your mouth shut and use this opportunity to make friends. Preferably friends whose parents are not only very wealthy, but also influential. You will pick your friends based on who their parents are. You will date boys based on who their parents are. You will stay out of trouble and play nice, even if they are wretched to you. And if a fat, pimply boy wants you to suck his small cock, you will do it if he's the son of a duke!" With a hard shake, she lets go of me, turns on her heels, and continues walking toward the front entrance of the school.

I rub my arms where her hands left red marks and glare at her retreating back in loathing. The one person I crave love and attention from is the one who refuses to give it to me. My mother has made it crystal clear that children are not her forte. Her attention has always been focused on who her next conquest was and how much they are worth. I was mostly raised by nannies and babysitters instead of an attentive mother. She has always been an opportunist, especially since she claims her one mistake in life was falling in love with my father.

She met him when she was a waitress at a high-end restaurant. He was a captain in the 1st Armoured Division in the British Army. His charm and good-looks were no match for my mother when he set his sights on her. She was pregnant within three months and they got married before my arrival. Right after my third birthday, he was deployed to Kuwait for the Gulf War and was a completely different man when he returned home six months later. The playful light that used to shine brightly from his green eyes was gone and in its place was fear, anxiety, and dread. Nightmares invaded his sleep and he turned to alcohol, hoping to forget his new memories from his time in the Persian Gulf. He was kicked out of the Army two months later for his PTSD diagnosis, sending him into a deeper spiral of depression.

My mother left him a short time later, bitterness forever in her veins from the loss of the man she once used to love.

Since her experience, my mother's advice is to never fall in love with good-looking men. "Make yourself come first, Cora," she warns me every time she finds herself single again. "Meet men who come from money. Use your beauty and charm them into marriage so that you can be taken care of for the rest of your life."

I take her advice with a grain of salt because turning out to be exactly like her is the *last* thing I want to happen. I just want to be loved, to finally get the attention that I feel I deserve.

So I decide to become an actress, a famous one at that.

Because I want the whole world to know who Cora Gregory is.

And I want them all to bend to *my* will.

I *want* the attention.

I *deserve* the attention.

I *will* get the attention.

The only redeeming quality about this boarding school is that they have an exceptional theatre program. With that reminder, I begrudgingly follow my mother to the entrance. One of these students must have a connection in the entertainment industry and I'm determined to find out who that is.

She presses the button on the intercom and announces herself when questioned by the voice through the speaker. A click and buzzing sound indicates that the door is now unlocked and we pull it open. We walk through the formal hall into the grand foyer, my eyes becoming wide at the chaotic scene of students in uniforms walking up and down the double staircases and through hallways to wherever their destinations might be. I take a deep breath and put on my mask of indifference as I catch men and women checking me out, whispering to themselves about the new stranger who has just entered their building.

A tall, lanky gentleman with a full head of gray hair in a brown suit walks toward us. "Welcome to Chackmore College, Mrs. Gregory. I am Headmaster Caldwell Aldrich and this is my assistant, Gretchen." My mother shakes both of their hands before their attention is drawn to me. "This must be Cora," he says as his brown eyes give me the once over, his head nodding in approval at my attire. My mother purposely bought us new dresses, coats, and boots for this visit, hoping we can fake the part of looking like we come from money.

"Why don't we go into my office so you can fill out paperwork while we discuss our expectations of Cora here at Chackmore?" He extends his arm out for us to follow Gretchen to their offices and I immediately feel bile start to rise up my throat at the thought of my mother leaving me here. Despite my hatred for her, at the end of the day, she is the only family I've got.

"Where is the loo … I mean, restroom?" I quickly correct myself as my mother gives me a murderous look for not using the proper term for a toilet.

"It is right over there." Gretchen points to a door along the wall behind me. "Why don't you just meet us in the office once you are done? It's the third door on the right." I nod my head in acknowledgement and quickly make my way to the bathroom. Once inside, I lock myself in a stall and try to control my rapid breathing, anxiety spreading into my lungs like smoke filling a burning building.

You will be just fine, Cora!

Think of it as the start of a new life!

You don't need your mother!

This is your chance to go for your dreams!

I repeat this to myself until I start to believe my own words. I take a deep breath, stand up and exit the stall. I wash my hands and look at myself in the mirror. I want to give myself a confident smile, but my mother tells me smiling increases wrinkles. Instead, I wink at my reflection, square my shoulders back, and hold my head high before turning around to exit the bathroom.

The foyer seems to be empty as I walk through it to go to the office, but a movement from the stairwell to my right catches my eye. Three boys descend the stairs, watching me. They look to be older, all of them with an athletic body. The hair on the back of my neck starts to rise and an uneasy feeling fills my veins with the way their mouths turn to sneers.

"Well, look what we have here, lads." They reach the bottom of the stairwell and surround me before I have a chance to pass them. They're tall and wearing their school uniforms of a navy blazer, yellow button-down shirt with a red tie, and khaki slacks.

"Looks like we have some fresh meat." A ginger haired boy to my left responds, his eyes raking over my body salaciously.

"Yes, and isn't she a pretty one!" I look to my right at a boy with black hair who starts to lick his lips, his eyes trained on my chest as my increased breathing draws attention to my breasts.

"What's your name, sweetheart?" The boy standing in front

of me asks. He could be considered good-looking with his blond hair and piercing light blue eyes, except I feel nothing but pure evil radiating off him.

"Cora!" I respond with a gasp of shock when my back hits the wall, not realizing I was walking backwards while they stalked toward me. I frantically look around for help, discouraged at the sight of two girls running by us.

"My name is Nate and these two here are Ed and Blake," the blond guy tells me, using his thumbs to indicate the other two boys. "If you do as we say and don't cause any trouble, we'll make sure your time here at Chackmore is … memorable," he laughs and the sound sends chills up my spine. He leans in close and whispers in my ear, "Do you like to share, Cora? Because we sure do." I recoil as he reaches out and traces his hand along my cheekbone.

"Looks like you're scaring her with your breath, Nate."

A voice coming from behind them has all three of them turning to look around at the two boys coming our way. But with the way Nate, Ed, and Blake back away from me once they recognize who it is, I can tell that these new guys are not part of their crowd.

"You're always so good at interrupting my fun, Harrington," Nate says sarcastically and the two new boys step in between us.

"We want no part of what you call fun," the other boy responds and I notice he has an Irish accent instead of an English one. The new guys block me in and stare down the other three boys. Ed and Blake refuse to meet their eyes and continue to move away from us.

"I don't give a fuck who your daddy is, Sean. He isn't here to protect you now," Nate sneers as he takes a step closer to Sean.

"Oh, but you should, Nate. Because of your last little stunt, you're skating on thin ice with Aldrich. It would only take one phone call from my father to tell him how you harassed a new student and we would say goodbye to your arse forever. So, I advise that you start making better choices and keep your hands to yourself."

Nate's jaw ticks and he slowly starts to walk away from us. "See you around, Cora," he taunts with a smirk and turns around to join the other boys. I breathe out a sigh of relief once I see them walk out of the hall.

"I'm going to follow them to make sure they don't come back," Sean tells the boy still standing in front of me, who nods in response. Sean looks at me and smiles, "Don't worry, lass, we will make sure they don't hurt you." He runs after them before I have a chance to thank him. *Remember his name*, I tell myself since not only did he come to my rescue, but Nate insinuated that this Sean fellow had a powerful father. I watch him walk out and notice that he has a decent body to go with his cute looks.

"Are you okay—Cora was it?" My attention is drawn to the boy now facing me and all thoughts of Sean completely vanish from my brain. My breath catches in my throat as my eyes behold his handsome face with aqua eyes that seem to want to read my soul. I swallow hard, trying to find my voice that his looks have robbed me of.

"Yes," I stutter. "My name is Cora. Yours?" I squeak out, needing to know the name of the man of my dreams.

He smiles and I suddenly feel lightheaded because I've never seen someone as beautiful as he. "My name is Cal. Cal Harrington," he says with pride, his strong voice soothing my rattled nerves. "That other guy is my best mate, Sean Lindsey. I promise that as long as we're around, we won't let Nate and his asshole friends hurt you. Just make sure you are never out walking alone, okay?"

He looks me up and down, noticing my attire. He raises one of his eyebrows in question. "Are you meeting with Headmaster Aldrich right now since you are not in uniform?"

"Yes, my mother is with him now. I was just on my way back to his office when those boys blocked my way there," I explain, hoping that Cal really means what he says when offering to protect me.

"Why don't I escort you back to his office?" He offers up his arm for me to take and all I can do is nod. He gives me another heart stopping smile and warning bells start to go off in my body as my mother's advice starts to blare in my head.

Never fall in love with a good-looking man, Cora!

But, it's now too late, as Cal Harrington has completely stolen my heart.

And I will stop at nothing to make him mine.

One

Cora

Present Day

I OPEN THE door to my apartment and sigh in relief to finally be back home. I just got off the plane from shooting my latest movie for the last three months in different locations around the world. Unfortunately, I only have a small amount of time before the press tour for another one of my movies begins. *At least I will be with Cal during this press tour,* I think and the thought makes me smile. I roll my suitcase into my bedroom and fall down onto my bed, exhaustion settling in.

What people don't understand or see is how utterly exhausting it is being an actress. Auditions, meetings, rehearsal, wardrobe changes, memorizing your lines, traveling, waiting around in your trailer, press releases, award shows … the list is endless. Thank goodness I was in the right place at the right time, vacationing with Cal and Sean during one of our school breaks, when all three of us were discovered by a talent scout. The talent scout got us in the door, but we have all had to work our asses off in order to keep ourselves in the business. All these years later, Cal and Sean are at the height of their careers while I still have to suck some director's cock in order to even be considered for a role. Not to mention, I'm still single, with Cal seeming to drift farther out of my reach.

"Damn you, Cal," I mutter out loud to no one but myself. I get up and off the bed to go straight to the kitchen to open a bottle of wine. Once I pour a large glass of Pinot Noir, I sit down and look at the view out of my living room window. A view that should've been London, but instead is a view of a nasty, dirty lake.

Lake Michigan in Chicago.

If you asked me where I thought I would be in my life right now, the answer would've been being Cal's wife and us living in London part time while we traveled the world together, taking turns shooting movies. I'm still striving for that kind of life, but instead, I'm living in a secret apartment that no one knows about in Chicago in order to follow his every move while he plays house with the mother of his children.

Never would I've imagined him falling in love with someone else. Nor would I've believed it would be with a commoner. I snort in disgust as an image of Jenna Pruitt comes to mind. I guess some might think she's pretty—if you think a fat mouse with beady, brown eyes is fucking pretty. I don't understand what he sees in her. And her body … *ugh!* She looks like a small man with her muscled arms and legs. Why any man likes an athletic body in a woman is beyond me. I keep myself lean and tight, with the help of Pilates, cigarettes, and cocaine. Food is a nuisance. I eat because I have to, but I try to get away with the bare minimum.

I shake my head, not understanding why this is happening to me. Jenna was only supposed to be a fling. I paid enormous amounts of money to people to help keep them apart. I thought I got rid of her until her out of control best friend drunkenly told a story involving a "secret" that Jenna was keeping. Turns out, that person she told was paparazzi and he sold the story for a lot of money.

A story whose secret was a child that Cal didn't know he even had.

A story that painted Cal's reputation as a deadbeat father.

I knew all about Cal's child before he did. I kept that secret because I knew if he found out, he would be lost to me forever. I thought I had borrowed time until the little brat was old enough to either want to find her daddy or want nothing to do with him. I was hoping Jenna would find someone else to be the kid's father. But four years later, that bitch was still not married and once the story became public, Cal immediately flew to Chicago to meet his daughter.

I didn't panic at first. During those four years, I spent as much time as I could with Cal. We made a movie together with Sean. We went on vacation together, we were each other's dates to movie premieres and we talked on the phone daily. I made sure to sabotage any other woman that came into his life before he could even really think about them. Fortunately, Cal is a workaholic and was determined to make a name for himself in Hollywood. He put dating on hold and I made myself available to him whenever he needed a date for any award ceremony, event, or even just to go out. We were photographed all the time together and I anonymously paid the press money to print stories about us secretly dating. As his fame rose, he barely paid attention to himself in the press and when his publicist brought the stories to his attention and asked if he wanted to issue a cease and desist for printing false information, he laughed it off and said he didn't care if they thought we were together.

That was when I knew I had chance.

I started to act more aggressive with him, more suggestive. He used to only look at me as a friend, but then one night at a party, he looked at me differently. The lust showed up in his eyes as his gaze lingered on my lips. Lips that I've been told look amazing wrapped around men's dicks. I was determined to have them wrapped around his that night. I proceeded to keep pumping him with alcohol as the taste of victory was near. When I saw he was teetering on the line between buzzed and inebriated, I made my move. I took him to a bathroom, locked the door and attempted to make him mine.

His lips were the most delicious lips I've ever tasted.

His tongue awakened a desire that no man has ever come close to making me feel.

He had me pinned to the wall, my legs wrapped around his waist, and I was *this close* to having him inside me, bare with no condom, when the banging on the door startled us apart. It was as if an ice-cold bucket of water was poured on him. He looked at me, saw the position we were in, and dropped me as if I burned him. He quickly buttoned up his pants and opened the door without saying a word and left.

Staring at me from the other side of that door was Sean Lindsey. The look of jealousy and desire shooting daggers at me from his eyes as he assessed the situation he just interrupted. Sean has loved me from the day he met me and I have used that love as a pawn in my game.

I keep him close so I can be close to Cal.

Sean and Cal have been best friends for years. There is no one who knows Cal better than Sean. I have toyed with the idea of Sean as my backup, but despite his good looks, Sean doesn't light my core on fire the way Cal does. So I keep Sean in my back pocket, teasing him with hope that one day we might be together.

Do I have remorse that I'm stringing him along? *Absolutely not!*

My mother taught me at a very young age to go after what I wanted, because the only person who can look out for me is me. And that's exactly what I'm doing.

I *want* Cal Harrington.

I will *have* Cal Harrington.

And *nobody* will stand in my way.

The ringing of my cell phone brings me out of my trance. I get up and retrieve it out of my purse to see my agent calling me. I purposely signed with Philip Logan because he was Cal and Sean's agent. He's ridiculously expensive, but worth every penny. I quickly debate whether or not to answer, but decide it's better to answer his call in order to see if I can get any information out of him regarding Cal's next movie.

"How is my favorite agent doing?" I sweetly ask when I answer the phone.

"Do you have another agent working for you? Because I wouldn't put that past you." His voice is sharp and angry, with no hint of amusement in it whatsoever. I sigh hearing his tone, knowing that this conversation will not be fun.

"What's wrong now, Philip?" I roll my eyes, not hiding my annoyance. I have no energy to deal with his melodrama today and I now regret answering his call.

"Guerdain is dropping you."

"*What?*" I screech, not expecting that kind of news. "They can't do that. I'm in a contract with them!" I have been the face of one of Guerdain's perfumes for the past five years, raking in a million dollars per year for my ad campaigns. They're my last endorsement since all of my other ones have run out and the companies don't want to renew. Some bullshit excuse saying I'm difficult to work with.

"They most certainly can and did, Cora. All you had to do was show up on time, be nice, and keep that pretty big mouth of yours shut! But it seems you not only were late this last photo shoot, but were rude to the director, whining about how slow he was and complaining about how long the shoot was. Your reputation is preceding you and no one wants to sign you anymore. I can't even get a tampon company to want you!" He sneers, making me want to hurl my phone against the floor and scream. I needed that money and with no other movies lined up right now, I need to figure out quickly what I'm going to do.

"What kind of scripts do you have for me, Philip?" I change the subject, hoping for some good news to come out of this conversation and that he has another job booked for me.

"I only have two scripts for you, but they are the same type of parts you seem to gravitate toward. Villainous bitch, ready to destroy things. I know those roles are true to reality, but aren't you tired of playing yourself?" His sarcasm makes me grit my teeth from refraining to tell him to go fuck himself.

"My fans like me in those roles and we want to keep them happy in order for them to keep going to the box office," I remind him so he can keep his focus on dollar signs and not the type of roles I play. "Scan and email the scripts to me so I can read them."

"Why don't I just physically hand them to you this weekend?"

"Since when were we meeting this weekend?" I ask in confusion, trying to remember if I agreed to a meeting in Los Angeles with him or if he was coming to London. My mother is the only one who knows about this apartment in Chicago, as the sneaky bitch went through my office in my London home and found the paperwork. Since her third divorce was finalized, I reluctantly agreed to let her live temporarily in my London home while I'm away in order for someone to take care of it. That was a year ago and it looks like she has no desire of ever leaving.

"Aren't you going to be at Cal's surprise birthday party?" His question stuns me into silence by this unexpected news. *What surprise party?* "Your silence leads me to believe that you didn't know about your supposedly *best friend's* party. Which means Jenna didn't invite you." He laughs and I wish I was physically in front of him to punch him in his smug, ugly face. "Can't blame her really since you make it painfully obvious how you want what is hers."

Fuck him! Cal is not hers.

"Do your job, Philip! Get me those scripts and find some more endorsement deals. I'll see you this weekend." I hang up on him and scream out my frustrations.

How dare that whore not invite me to his birthday party! I start pacing my living room, frantically thinking of ways to crash the party when I immediately think of Sean and dial his phone number.

"Hello, handsome," I purr when he answers. "Am I going to see you this weekend? I really miss you." I lower my voice so that it sounds husky and genuine.

"Sorry, Cora, but I'm not in London," he tells me, his voice sounding distant as if he's uninterested in talking to me. "I will ring you when I return."

"I know you're in Chicago for the big party, Sean. I was thinking I can come with you and be your plus one," I reply nonchalantly, trying to act calm.

"I know firsthand that you weren't invited, Cora. How do you even know about it?" He questions, but his voice is laced with amusement and I relax hearing hints of how he normally sounds when talking with me.

"It doesn't matter how I found out. What matters is that I'm there with you, celebrating our oldest friend. Don't you think Cal would be upset if one of his best friends wasn't there? Besides, it would be nice to have some alone time with you. Just like old times," I imply with purpose, hoping to jog his memory of the good times we recently had together.

All three of us reunited last year to shoot the sequel to our highly successful drama thriller we made five years ago. With Jenna always being on set, I spent most of my free time with Sean. But even he couldn't distract me from my anger at having to see *her* every day with the man that's supposed to be mine.

"I don't know what Cal thinks anymore since his head is so far up Jenna's ass. No offense, but he probably wouldn't even notice if you weren't there."

Despite his joking tone, his words make me seethe. *How dare he throw that in my face!* I mentally count to ten to calm down before responding to him.

"Sean, I want to see you and I know you want to see me too. I will text you on Friday when I land so you can let me know what hotel to meet you at."

"I'm staying with Cal and Jenna. Since you're going to be a party crasher, might be best if you stay at a hotel, Cora."

"Fine, but you're always welcome to share my room if the baby keeps you awake," I suggest, giving Sean the option of choosing me instead of being in a house with gross, stinky children. Jenna gave birth to their son, Brooks, who just turned one. Another party that I wasn't invited to. I shake off my bitterness to focus back on the conversation.

"Text me when you land, Cora. We can make plans then. I need to go." I stare at the phone in shock when I see he hung up on me without saying goodbye.

I walk into my bedroom, pull open the closet doors, and start sifting through my clothes. All my clothes here are dull and boring. Most of them having to be a disguise so I don't get recognized. I grab my red wig, go into my bathroom, and look at myself as I put it on and adjust it to properly fit my head.

"Sean is dead wrong if he thinks Cal won't notice me at his party," I say to my reflection with an evil smile. Satisfied with my appearance, I give myself a wink of confidence and leave my room to grab my purse and sunglasses.

It's time to go shopping for a dress that will make sure no one forgets my attendance at Cal's party.

Two

Sean

"TALKING WITH YOUR she-devil?"

I spin around in surprise at the sound of Jenna's voice. So engrossed was I in my thoughts over my conversation with Cora that I didn't hear her approach the kitchen. She's leaning against the doorframe, arms crossed against her chest, looking at me with annoyance.

Fuck, she wasn't supposed to hear anything. I quickly place my phone in the back pocket of my jeans to try to hide it. I'm the dumbass who took the phone call in *her* kitchen instead of going outside, so it's just my luck that she would hear my conversation. Not really wanting to reveal the news about Cora's future attendance in her home, I give her my best, innocent smile and decide to deflect the question.

"Jenna, dear, don't you know it's not nice to sneak up on people while they're having a conversation? Now I see where your daughter gets it from."

Jenna and Cal's daughter, Avery, is notorious for sneaking up on people and hearing inappropriate conversations at the wrong time. At the tender age of eight, she has already heard about cum juice and butt plugs.

"But I'll forgive you for scaring me since you look so ravishing in your sweaty workout attire," I tell her with a wink.

She rolls her eyes at my flirtatious banter and moves away from the doorframe to the refrigerator.

I can't help my eyes from scanning her tight body, clad in black work out leggings and a loose fitting white t-shirt. Since having their second child, Jenna has been working hard to make sure she maintains her pre-baby shape. I scan her face while she pulls out a water bottle from the refrigerator and takes a deep gulp from it. Her face is looking a little too thin, making me wonder if she's becoming obsessed with keeping herself in shape. I make a mental note to talk to Cal about it when she interrupts my thoughts with her next words.

"Give me one good reason why I shouldn't kick you out of my house for inviting her to Cal's party?" Her whiskey-colored eyes shoot daggers at me in anger. Her tone of voice is harsh, but the underlying hint of hurt is clearly detectable. Now I'm the asshole for betraying her.

Bloody fucking hell, she did hear everything! Jenna is one of the last people I want to upset. Not only because she's my best friend's fiancée, but also because I love her like a sister. She has been brutally honest with me about her feelings for Cora since Cora has made her dislike for Jenna clear from the moment Jenna entered Cal's life. What endears Jenna the most to me is that she isn't worried about herself, but more concerned about me and my feelings for Cora.

Feelings that I had for her since the moment I laid eyes on her in boarding school.

Feelings that have never been reciprocated.

Feelings that I tried to turn off for years, but managed to come back alive as if I'm hit with a bolt of lightning every time I saw her or heard her voice.

Feelings that I know will never be returned back to me.

"I didn't invite her, Jenna. She already knew about it. The only person who could have told her would have been Philip," I remind her, hoping that her anger will shift from me toward him.

"Yet you did nothing to discourage her from coming," she

counters back, slamming the water bottle against the kitchen counter.

I narrow my eyes at her, not liking her tone of voice with me. "I don't appreciate having my private phone conversations being listened to, Jenna."

"Then don't have your private conversations in *my* kitchen, Sean!" She emphasizes and we just stare at each other in silence. I'm the first one to break our gaze as I rake my hands through my hair and sigh in defeat. She's right—I could have told Cora no and I didn't. Instead I let her get her way … as usual.

"I'm sorry, Jenna. I didn't think of how her being at Cal's party would upset you since she has been a longtime friend of his. I promise I will control her and make sure she doesn't cause trouble," I offer, not wanting to fight with Jenna. It's for the best that I acknowledge that I'm in the wrong.

She looks at me in disbelief, a bitter laugh escaping her. "You can't control Cora Gregory, Sean. If anything, she controls *you*." She walks toward me, stops directly in front of me and pokes her finger into my chest. Jenna's petite, standing at only five feet three inches tall, so she has to lean her head back in order to look me in the eyes since I stand a foot above her. "Keep her away from me and my children, Sean, and we'll have a great night."

"I will try my best, Jenna," I tell her with fake reassurance, not feeling confident at all about the task. Keeping Cora from trying to talk with Cal is going to be tricky since Cal's usually glued to Jenna's side at all times. Keeping Cora away from both of them will be challenging.

Who am I kidding? It won't happen.

As if Jenna can read my mind, she looks at me with disappointment and shakes her head. She tries to walk around me to leave, but I grab her arm instead and turn her back to me.

"What, Jenna? Why the look?" Sometimes disappointing Jenna feels worse than disappointing my own parents.

"I just don't get it, Sean. You're one of the biggest movie stars in the world, who can have any woman they want, and yet you are in love with a snake."

"Being a bit dramatic now, aren't we?" I tease in amusement at her calling Cora a snake.

"I don't think so, Sean. She has been in love with your best friend since the day you two entered her life. You know it and yet you continue to let her manipulate and use your feelings for her so she can try to get closer to him."

I look at her in stone-cold silence, her words like little knives slicing at my heart.

Because deep down, I know she's right.

"She's evil, Sean. She was born that way and will never change."

"No one is born evil, Jenna," I interrupt, tired of hearing her opinions on Cora. Regardless of my feelings for Cora, she's still one of my closest friends. "Cora just wants to be loved. She never got that from her parents and unfortunately, is looking for it in the wrong places."

"When are you going to stop making excuses for her, Sean?" Jenna pleads as she grabs my hands and squeezes them. "Why can't you move on to someone who will love you as much as you love them? You deserve that, Sean!"

"You're right, I do, but how does one go about dating when they are a celebrity? Online dating? Going to the pubs? Maybe I should just take random trips every week to see if I get the chance to meet a beautiful lady in first class." I give her a knowing smile, referencing at how she met Cal.

She can't help the blush that creeps up her face as she reminisces of that airplane ride. "I don't know, but Cora Gregory is not the love of your life. You just haven't realized that yet. Until then, we need to figure out how to get you back in the dating world." She turns to leave, but then pauses and turns back to me. "Dating, Sean, not just fucking."

"What a dirty little mouth for such a prestigious lady," I tease, thoroughly enjoying when Jenna curses since it's such a rarity. But Jenna barely acknowledges me as she's deep in thought of how I should meet the future Mrs. Sean Lindsey.

"You need someone who is smart, with a quick wit, and a strong tongue to handle your charm."

"I like the strong tongue part. Oral skills are very important." I throw my head back in laughter at the look of disgust that Jenna gives me. "Get your mind out of the gutter, Jenna! Of course I meant oral as in how she verbally communicates." She rolls her eyes at my lie and is about to say something back when our attention is diverted to the window at the sound of children's laughter.

We both walk over to see Isla, Jenna's nanny, playing with Avery and Brooks in the pool. Isla is standing on the steps of the pool, holding Brooks on her hip, while laughing as Avery splashes them from doing a cannon ball into the pool. I take in the tiny, blue string bikini Isla is wearing and immediately feel my dick stirring.

Calm down, boy. Isla is off limits!

Isla Jones has been in my life as long as I can remember, with our parents being friends before we were born. We have shared numerous holidays together, with most of my memories of Isla being that annoying little sister who wouldn't stop following my brothers and me around. With her being six years younger than us, we were never interested in playing with her, and I barely paid attention to her when she came to visit. Once I went away to England for boarding school, I hadn't seen Isla in years. She then went away to school and was living in Paris for work after she graduated. When Cal and Jenna were looking for a nanny, I casually asked my mother if she knew of anyone, not even thinking about Isla. I was pleasantly surprised to hear that she was available since the last time I had heard news about her, it was of her employment as a nanny for some children of a French dignitary. So when I saw her for the first time as Cal and Jenna's nanny at an event in Vancouver, I barely recognized her. Shock is not even the proper word I would use for my reaction at seeing her for the first time after all these years.

Because annoying little Izzy had turned into a beautiful woman who only answers to the name of Isla.

A woman who captivates most men's attention anywhere she goes, without even trying.

And I was astonished at how my body instantly reacted to her.

Desire and want flooded through my veins the second her eyes connected with mine.

No, this can't be Izzy, I had thought. For a brief second, I thought it was Cora since they both have the similar hair and eye color, but then I realized it wasn't by dress she was wearing. Cora was at the same event with me, so I knew it couldn't be her. When I analyzed her more closely, I realized that the gorgeous stranger was my Izzy.

Izzy's blond hair had turned darker, into more of a mocha color. She lost her adolescent chubbiness and her face became slender with high cheekbones and her green eyes captivating me. Her body morphed into a work of art from Michelangelo himself. Watching her now in her bathing suit, my hands itch to cup her perky, full breasts, while her long legs make me daydream about them being wrapped around my waist.

How could I be thinking this way of little Izzy?

I wouldn't be a hot-blooded male if I *didn't* think this way about Isla.

As I give my head a good shake and come back to reality, I turn to notice that Jenna has been watching me with a disapproving look that screams *I know who you've been thinking about!*

"I think we need to cool off from your work out. Fancy a swim?" I nod toward the pool and wiggle my eyebrows.

"We?" she asks suspiciously. "Touch my nanny, Sean, and I will chop off your balls." She huffs at my mischievous smile, turns on her heel, and walks out of the kitchen. I chuckle to myself at how astute Jenna is while I make my way to their guest bedroom to change into swim trunks.

Because I have no plans on staying away from Isla Jones.

Three

Isla

THE HAIRS ON the back of my neck rise, my body sensing him before even seeing him.

His husky laughter at something Cal tells him as they walk along the side of the pool makes my insides clench at the sexiness of it.

Don't look, Isla. Concentrate on the children.

But when it comes to Sean Lindsey, the man has always commanded my attention.

He had been the center of my universe ever since I was a child when I was in love with him, only to have him continuously break my heart every time he ignored me.

Little Izzy. I despised that name and loathed it even more when he sneered it in his adolescent teasing way when we were growing up. He always saw me more as a nuisance since I was the only girl amongst all boys.

Yet I saw him as a God.

As years went by and we went off to our respective schools, our family visits became few and far between. My schoolgirl crush on him lessoned as I grew older and when I started to receive attention from other guys, Sean became a distant memory.

But a memory that, nonetheless, managed to still turn up in my dreams.

I try not to watch his magnificent body saunter over to a lawn chair to sunbathe, but my eyes are glued to the hard roundness of his delectable ass. Thank goodness I'm wearing sunglasses so I can tilt my head one way, while admiring the view out of my peripheral vision.

His chiseled chest and abs are covered with a small sampling of hair. His bicep muscles are defined and toned to be the perfect size, with his left bicep wrapped in a unique tattoo. I'm not usually attracted to men with tattoos, but his suits him. As if I'm watching a movie in slow motion, he meticulously slathers his body in sunscreen, making sure he doesn't miss a spot. A devil of a smile plays on his lips as if he knows he's being watched. I shake my head and turn my back toward him, marveling at the fact that he keeps getting better looking with age.

It isn't fair that men are made to look like Sean Lindsey. His handsomeness is at a level that few can even match. Unfortunately, his attitude is exactly what one would assume one who looks like him would be—cocky, arrogant, egotistical, and can charm your panties right off of you within a blink of an eye. My brothers would talk about Sean's reputation with envy and I would get mildly irritated at hearing about his conquests.

Learning that he was in love with an evil bitch like Cora Gregory was downright devastating.

He revealed that information to my brothers one drunken night years ago when we were all home in Ireland together. After the initial shattering of my heart at this news, my agony quickly turned into disgust because I couldn't understand how someone as intelligent as Sean could ever fall for a selfish, narcissistic woman. He had brought her home during the holidays numerous times, claiming she had nowhere to go since her home life wasn't a healthy environment. Both of our families welcomed her with open arms and she played the part by being on her best behavior, but I would see that glint of malevolence shimmering from her eyes at me, especially any time someone commented on how much we resembled each other. Sure, we both have dark, brown hair and green eyes, but that is where the similarities end. I don't walk around with permanent resting bitch face and a stick up my ass. I would always pray that the clouds would be lifted from Sean's eyes and he would see how wrong she was for him. *How could he want her when she doesn't even hide her lust for Cal, his own best friend?* But, judging from the way he looked at her when I last saw them on set of the movie that the three of them were shooting together, his feelings for her haven't changed.

His weakness for someone who is so wrong for him makes me realize that Sean is not the strong-minded man I viewed him to be. Combined with my former employer trying to sexually assault me while I slept, my views on men and love are no longer childhood fairytales.

No man will define who I am and what I do with my life.

Life is not a love song where the girl and boy meet and fall in love. Life is hard, messy, beautiful and can be downright nasty. I'm the only one who can make myself happy. Men are just the icing on the cake.

I can't be in love with someone like Sean, but he can be my current object of desire, wrapped up in an invisible bow with a big warning sign saying, "Stay far, far away." I see the way he's been looking at me these past two months that he's been staying here and it's anything but brotherly. I secretly enjoy seeing his eyes graze over my body, liking what he sees so that he has to physically adjust himself. It's satisfying to know that I finally got his attention, but what good is it if he still wants Cora?

Doesn't mean that I can't still have fun with him. It has been close to three years since my last boyfriend, with only casual dating in between. I *crave* physical contact and when my gaze returns to the man of my thoughts, an idea starts to form.

I'm an adult now. I can totally take my emotions out of the equation and have a casual fling with Sean until he leaves.

No, you can't! My heart screams.

You are a strong, independent woman! You can definitely handle it! My brain inserts.

Get him inside you now! My vagina demands as it clenches every time I feel his heated, intense stare on me.

"Uncle Robert!" Avery's sweet little voice interrupts my thoughts and I give a silent prayer of thanks for her distraction. I turn around to see Jenna's assistant, Robert, walk from the patio doors toward us. I'm shocked to see him in a swimsuit since it's the middle of the day during the work week, but working for Jenna Pruitt comes with a lot of perks. One of them being a flexible schedule and working from home—or in this case, from her pool. He puts his laptop down on the table and joins us by sitting next to me on the stairs in the pool.

"I have an observation," he says, his voice low so no one can hear him. His head is positioned straight, looking at where Cal and Sean are sitting, but with his aviator sunglasses shielding his eyes, I'm unsure as to who he's really looking at.

"And what is that?" I ask in anticipation since I always enjoy listening to Robert's gossip, especially when it's usually things about life in Hollywood that his boyfriend, Kellan, tells him. Kellan is Cal's stylist, but he also styles other big names in Hollywood. He's based in Los Angeles, but they make their long-distance relationship work by flying out to see each other every other weekend.

"The yards of fabric on your bathing suit seem to be shrinking in the presence of Mr. Lindsey." He turns his attention toward me, one eyebrow raised in mock questioning with a smirk playing across his lips.

"You're so ridiculous, Robert. When was the last time you even saw me in a bathing suit?" I question, my voice bored with his observation already. If he's right, it was not intentionally done. I needed new bathing suits and since I always see Jenna wearing her bikinis when she swims, I didn't think it was a big deal if I wore mine.

"Last week you were wearing a tankini. Today you're wearing four small triangles that leave little to the imagination. You're lucky Jenna doesn't feel threatened by you wearing that around

Cal." His voice turns serious and I gasp in shock. I look down at myself and realize that Robert is right, this is *not* an appropriate bathing suit for a nanny to be wearing. Guilt floods through me and my cheeks feel like they are burning from embarrassment.

"Oh my gosh, I need to go change. I don't want to do anything that upsets Jenna!"

Sometimes I forget that Jenna is actually my boss because from day one, she has welcomed me with open arms and treats me more like her little sister. Cal is the only one who still intimidates me when he stares at you, which he does to everyone with no shame. It feels as if he's sizing everyone up, assessing if he feels you're worthy to be around Jenna and their children, much less him. He treats me with professionalism and barely speaks to me, letting Jenna be the one in charge of running the household.

"Changing would be too obvious. Calm down, you're fine." He dismisses the subject with a wave of his hand.

I get up and walk down the pool steps, clutching Brooks tighter to me while we move deeper into the water in hopes that it covers most of my body. Brooks squeals in delight as the water covers him, kicking his chunky little legs around. I stop when the depth of the water touches underneath my breasts. I hear water rustling behind me and know Robert is following me.

"Oh yeah, that thing is barely covering your T&A." His shades fall down to the tip of his nose as he looks up from my ass and stares at my tits.

"What is T&A?" Avery questions, coming up behind Robert. A high-pitched squeal comes out of him, making both kids laugh. We were so engrossed in our conversation that we didn't notice Avery swimming toward us. I give him an evil smile since it seems that once again, Avery hears something inappropriate coming out of his mouth. I can't wait to see how he tries to get out of this one.

"Avery! You scared me!" He slaps his hand over his heart dramatically. "Why are you not wearing your bell?"

Robert gave Avery a small bell on a silver chain as a present to wear so he can hear when she's around. It was more of a present for him so he would stop getting in trouble with Cal and Jenna when they hear Avery repeating the not-suited-for-children comments that come out of his mouth in almost every conversation he engages in.

"I can't wear a bell in the pool, Uncle Robert." She looks at him as if he's crazy and I can't help the snort that escapes me. At eight years old, Avery's as sassy as her mother and questions everything that comes out of anyone's mouth, because her attitude is already one of a know-it-all.

"That bell is your new jewelry and needs to be on you at all times. Even in the shower!" He points his finger at her, which only gets him rewarded with an eye roll from her.

"What is T&A and why is it covering Izzy?" She asks once again and the look in her eyes is one of sheer determination. She will not stop asking until she gets an answer.

Robert sees it, but instead of looking panicked, he briefly glances at me with a wicked smile before grabbing Avery underneath her arms to bring her closer to him for a hug.

"T&A stands for Tadas and Awesomeness and that's what Izzy is covered in." I bite the inside of my cheek to refrain from laughing at Robert's clever answer. "Don't you think Izzy is awesome? And isn't 'ta-da' one of your favorite words to say?" She nods her head in response.

"You know who is also pretty awesome?" Robert continues, giving me a mischievous side-eye. "Your mommy! So when you see her next, you should tell her that she is all T&A." He starts to tickle Avery and I groan out loud in exasperation at him for continuing to cause trouble.

"Robert…" I slowly warn and try to give him a stern look, but fail miserably. The image of Avery innocently telling Jenna that she is all tits and ass without knowing what it stands for is quite comical.

"Just keeping everyone on their toes here, Isla," he jokes

before putting Avery down and leaving the pool in order to answer his ringing cell phone that's on the table by his laptop.

I shake my head at his retreating back and smile because he does contribute to the awesomeness of the gig. Robert has become a friend, showing me around Chicago and taking me to all of the local popular hangouts on my days off. Even Jenna will drop the kids off at her parents' house and take me for a girls only dinner when Cal is out of town. Because of everyone's warmth and kindness, I have not felt homesick yet in over a year since being employed by them.

A shout and a loud splash makes me whip my head around to see that Sean and Cal dove into the pool and are now swimming toward us in a race. I grab Avery's arm and narrowly miss being taken out by Cal, who touches the side of the pool only a fraction of a second before Sean does.

"Yeah, Daddy won!" Avery claps her hands in excitement as Cal reaches for her.

"It was the sight of you and your mommy that made me want to get to this side of the pool as fast as I could." He kisses her cheek and hands her over to Sean, who places her on his back so they can dive underwater together. Brooks starts splashing his arms around, his gurgling baby noises growing louder when he notices his mother. Jenna is now outside, looking over Robert's shoulder as he shows her something on his laptop. He says something that makes her laugh and she slaps his shoulder before walking toward the pool.

Robert and Jenna have been through a lot together and it is obvious in the way they handle their relationship, both personally and professionally. There's a lot of respect for one another, as well as a lot of love because they bicker and banter as if they were siblings. As Jenna's event planning company has thrived throughout the years, she has made sure Robert has grown with it. She has given him the keys to her kingdom now, trusting him without hesitation to run it. The company has become so successful under his leadership that big name corporations have recently been offering Jenna millions of dollars to buy it from her. She hasn't talked much about it, but with the addition of Brooks to the family, and her and Cal agreeing to not be away from each other for more than two weeks while he's on location, I suspect that Jenna might be considering one of those offers.

As she makes her way to the pool, her eyes are solely locked on Cal. A seductive smile is playing across her lips and her eyes are telling him secrets that only he can decode. He waits for her at the stairs, looking at her as a lion watches his prey. Hunger, heat—it radiates from him while his gaze trails up and down her body. The way they stare at each other makes me blush, but I can't seem to look away as envy burns inside me.

He holds out his hand for her as she walks down the stairs into the pool. As soon as she's within reach, he wraps his arms around her, placing one hand possessively on her ass, the other behind her neck so he can crush her mouth to his. Her legs immediately wrap around his waist, her arms going around his neck and her hands hold onto his head while his mouth devours hers. Tongues plunge into each other's mouths and it's clear that they don't care if they have an audience. Watching them makes me realize that my earlier thinking of a casual fling is not really what I want.

I want a man to look at me the way Cal looks at Jenna.

I want to find a love that makes me feel crazy drunk without any drops of alcohol.

I want a man to consume me the way he consumes her.

Starting an affair with Sean Lindsey will not get me any of these things.

"I predict Baby Harrington #3 in ten months' time," Robert remarks while making his way back to the pool. Jenna and Cal break their kiss, her cheeks red with embarrassment. Cal brings them down into the water as Jenna tries to break away from him, but he hauls her back against his chest.

"No!" Jenna sternly says, shaking her head at Robert.

"*Yes!*" Cal groans seductively, pressing his forehead into

hers. He leans in to whisper something in her ear that makes her laugh. It has gotten silent, their laughter the only noise filling the air. Robert is watching them with the same dewy expression that I probably have on my face. I feel the sensation that someone is watching me and I look over to see Sean holding Avery on his hip. Avery is watching her parents with a look of disgust on her face due to boys currently having the cooties, but it's Sean who draws my attention. I feel waves of desire pulsating off of him, his penetrating gaze like an electrical current that's making its way toward me and causing the pool to all of a sudden feel like a hot tub. His beautiful full lips are slightly parted, making it seem like he's having difficulty breathing. I zero in on those lips, wondering if they feel as soft as they look. My eyes make their way up to his, only to notice that he's not looking right at me, but at my chest. I look down to find the left triangle of my bikini pushed aside and being fisted into a small little hand.

Brooks has exposed my breast, his tiny fist positioned so that it's covering up my nipple.

I gasp out in horror and try to pry the material out of his hand, but his death grip on it only tightens. He starts to move his fists in anger at having to let go of what seems to become a comfort to him. I try to bring him closer so that his body is covering my now exposed nipple, but he starts to squirm away from me.

"Let me help you with that." Sean let's go of Avery and makes his way toward me in determination to get a closer look, his eyes still glued to my breast.

"No!" I cry out and turn my back to him. "Please let go, Brooks!" I try to say in a soothing voice, but soon his hands grab at my actual nipple and pull, causing me to yelp out in pain. Jenna races over to take Brooks, who happily frees himself from my boob in order to be in her arms. I pant out in pain as I quickly cover myself up, pressing my palm against the throbbing to make sure my nipple is still intact.

"I'm so sorry, Isla! I should've warned you that Brooks did that to me last week, hence why I went out and bought this new bathing suit." Her new bikini top is a sports performance halter top, leaving it impossible for any boob exposure.

"I'm going to go change," I whisper in mortification and refuse to look her in the eyes.

I feel her hand on my shoulder, which forces me to glance at her. "Why don't you just start your night off early?" Her look of sympathy makes me want to crawl into bed and never come out again.

I nod and make my way out of the pool, refusing to look back at Sean, who I feel watching my departure. I glance up to see Robert holding a towel out for me. He's biting on his lower lip to refrain from laughing, his look of '*I told you so*' making me want to smack the smug expression off his face.

"Fuck off!" I hiss at him, making sure my voice was low enough for his ears only. I tune out his chuckle as I walk briskly into the house. I grab an ice pack from the refrigerator and run to my bedroom to nurse my wounded nipple in what has turned out to be one of the most embarrassing moments of my life.

Four

Sean

BROOKS HARRINGTON IS my hero.

Yes, babies can be heroes and his groping skills today gave me a front row seat to the unveiling of Isla's silky, creamy, glorious breast. A stunning vision that has stayed with me well after I jerked off to the memory of it and all the things I want to do to it.

I want to caress her beautiful bud of a nipple between my fingers.

I want to squeeze the roundness of her breast to see if it fits my hand as perfectly as I imagine it will.

I want to suck and lick her to see if she tastes as good as I think she will.

Just thinking of her again makes me uncomfortably hard in the confine of my jeans. I go back into my bathroom to splash my face with cold water, hoping it will help me calm down. But after today, the only thing that's going to help me is finally tasting what I've been craving.

Isla Jones needs to be mine.

Long term? No, I just need a sampling and then be on my merry way, especially since my time in Castle Harrington is coming to an end soon. I don't even know why I've stayed as long as I have.

Stop lying to yourself, Sean. You know exactly why.

My why is that I'm fucking lonely.

And I want exactly what Cal has—a life partner who supports and worships me.

There, I admit it.

I know all about my reputation–they call me the *Irish Playboy*– and I've done nothing to squash those rumors. I've hung out with every new starlet that pops up in Hollywood. I dated the seasoned good girls of Hollywood. I've fucked my share of Hollywood royalty and it wasn't because I was interested in getting to know them.

I fuck other women to pacify my ego.

An ego that's damaged by the one woman I loved who doesn't want me.

Getting laid was never the initial reasoning for becoming an actor. My father was a famous politician back home in Ireland. Following in his footsteps was the last thing I wanted to do. I wanted to make a name for myself and not only being known as Alistair Lindsey's son. So when fate put a casting agent in my path during a holiday break, I jumped at the opportunity he was willing to give me. And the domino effect began.

Want to pay me to be a thief in a movie? Sign me up!

Want to pay me to blow up shit? I will sign on the dotted line.

Want to pay me to be the guy every woman falls in love with in a romantic comedy? I'm ready, eager, and willing.

RomComs have become one of my favorite movies to shoot. They're usually short, easy scripts to memorize, the female lead is always good-looking, and they pay almost as much as the big blockbuster blow up movies.

What I wasn't expecting was wanting to actually become *that* guy.

The asshole playboy who turns out to get his happily ever after.

And that's exactly what I want.

I was wishing for Cora to be my happily ever after, but I

don't even recognize the woman she has become today. She has always been a little rough around the edges due to her unhappy childhood, but Cal and I were always privy to see the fun, adventurous, and silly side to her. I knew she required to be center of attention, but I was always willing to give her that. I was hoping her crush on Cal was just a phase, especially when it was *I* who was always bailing her out of trouble, taking her out, giving her money when she said she was broke, and buying her nice presents. I made my desire for her crystal clear and when she said she wasn't ready, I told her I would give her time.

But then the rumors of her sucking directors' off to land roles reached my ears and I became enraged. I ignored her phone calls and refused to see her. I slept with any woman who smiled my way, hoping to make Cora jealous to realize what she was missing out on.

A man who would love her unconditionally.

A man who would take care of her forever.

It wasn't until Jenna came into Cal's life that Cora changed for the worse. The light that I used to see shine in her eyes when she was happy is gone and is replaced with a dark, anxiety ridden edge to her. She's secretive, demanding, and has created a horrible reputation for herself in the industry.

As her friend, I'm worried for her. But I have to stop making Cora a priority in my life and start putting myself first.

I have to stop trying to save someone who doesn't want to be saved.

It's time to let her go.

Damn it if that's not easier said than done. All that woman had to do was give me a come-hither look and my dick sprang into action, making me act like a love sick fucking fool. And that's another reason I've been staying at Cal's for the last two months as well. I'm hiding here, trying to sort my feelings out when it pertains to her. When all three of us were filming our movie together last year, it felt like old times while the cameras were rolling. But as soon as the director would call it a day,

Cal went to his trailer where Jenna and the kids were waiting for him, leaving Cora and I alone together. We did everything together–eating our meals, practicing lines, going out. We were companions in every sense of the word except for the physical part. Not that I didn't try, but all I ever got was a kiss. Still, I saw fleeting glimpses of the girl I fell in love with, giving my heart hope that she's still in there and I can pull her out.

But her obsession with Cal is making me realize that she was never mine to have.

I stare at myself in the mirror after drying my face off. *When the fuck are you going to wake up, Sean?* If I want what Cal has, I need to start finding the right woman because clearly, Cora is not it. I owe it to myself to start investing some time into meeting someone new. But while I start searching, what's the harm in having a little fun with a beautiful woman who I already know and is living under the same roof as me?

I look at my watch to see that it's past dinner time. Jenna keeps the children on a pretty strict dinner and bedtime schedule. As I exit my bedroom to head toward the dining room, I decide that I'll stay here until it's time for Cal and me to leave for the press tour for our movie from last year. That gives me one month until I have to spend numerous amounts of time with Cora again and enough time to continue working on myself.

One month is also enough time to woo Isla Jones into my bed.

Satisfied with my plan, I arrive in the dining room to find Cal, Jenna, and their children almost done with their dinner. Not wanting to be questioned on my whereabouts, I quickly sit down and dive right into the plate that was left for me.

"How are my girls doing?" I ask, looking at Avery and Jenna. I look around the room to see that Isla and Robert are missing from dinner. "Where is everyone?"

"Who do you precisely mean?" Jenna gives me a direct look, her eyes daring me to say who I'm thinking.

"Where's Robert?" I give her an innocent smile, challenging her by raising my eyebrows. She rolls her eyes at me and continues feeding Brooks his pureed baby food that is neon green. I shudder at it, knowing that's exactly what his diapers probably look like as well after consuming the homemade baby food Jenna makes herself. As much as I love Brooks, diapers are not my thing.

"Uncle Robert went home," Avery answers while she watches me cut into my skirt steak. Avery has become a vegetarian like her mother, the thought of eating animals making her turn up her cute little button nose at you. I deliberately cut my steak slower, slather the piece of meat in its juices before I bring it up to my mouth. Her eyes are as round as saucers, her face contorted in horror as I close my eyes and moan in pleasure at the deliciousness of it.

"You are eating a cow, Uncle Sean," she whispers and for a fleeting moment, I feel like an asshole for teasing her with my food.

"Don't worry, my little lass, I won't be mooing anytime soon." I give her a wink and look over at Cal to laugh with him, thinking he would find the whole thing funny. Instead his expression is one of murder for messing with his baby girl.

"Avery, we don't insert our opinions into other people's lives, especially when it pertains to food," Jenna chides and now I really am a bastard for getting her in trouble.

"But Mommy, he's eating a cow! I just love him so much that I don't want him to get E. coli!" She hysterically exclaims, tears threatening to spill from her aqua eyes. We all can't help but laugh at how adorable she is and that she even knows what E. coli means. She just gutted me with her sweetness, making me hope that one day I have a beautiful little girl who loves me as much as Avery does.

"I'm sorry, lass," I murmur as I lean into her. I kiss her cheek and swipe away at the lone tear that slides down. "Do you forgive me? Because I love you so much and I promise I didn't mean to get you in trouble."

She takes a shaky breath and sighs, showing signs of an

actress in the making. She nods and says, "I forgive you," with a serious tone to her little voice. I bite my lip to keep my laughter at bay and pull her into my lap for a hug. I push my plate away from her so she wouldn't have to look at my half-eaten steak. Jenna stands up and hands Brooks to Cal while she starts to gather the dirty plates.

"Avery, where is your nanny tonight?" I whisper in her ear while watching Jenna's retreating back into the kitchen.

"That's none of your business!" Jenna yells, not even turning back to look at me. *Damn her superwoman hearing!*

"Isla gets Wednesday nights off if we are home," Cal responds, his eyes questioning me.

"But she has been here most Wednesday nights for dinner." I rack my brain, trying to remember a Wednesday night I didn't see her while I've been here and I come up empty. Unless she's traveling with Jenna and Cal, Isla is always at dinner with us. Even on Sundays, her day off.

"She usually doesn't take it off," Cal shrugs, his attention on Brooks as he nuzzles underneath his neck in order to make him laugh.

"She's going out with Uncle Robert to get laid."

We hear a horrified gasp, signaling that Jenna's arrival back into the conversation seems to be just as perfect as her daughter's intrusion into other people's conversations. I stare silently at Cal, who looks between Avery and Jenna, his eyes rapidly blinking, trying to process what he just heard come out of his precious daughter's mouth.

"Avery, it's time to get ready for bed," Jenna says, her voice calm, but her eyes wild with shock. She shakes her head no at Cal as she takes Brooks from him, silently commanding that he not bring it up when he looks as if he's about to speak.

"Okay, Mommy." Avery kisses both Cal and I on the cheek goodnight and takes her mother's hand to be led upstairs. They leave in silence but not before we hear Avery ask, "Mommy, what does 'get laid' even mean?"

To my disappointment, I can't hear Jenna's response as they get farther away from the dining room. I lean back in my chair and look at Cal in bemusement as he just sits there with a dazed expression on his face.

"I think I'm going to have to start dying my hair soon since I'll be gray at a young age due to my daughter." He shakes his head as we both are now able to laugh at the situation.

"That girl is the best, but you *are* in a lot of trouble when she's older," I warn with sincerity. Avery is a beautiful child, who is going to grow into a gorgeous woman. With her looks and her mother's sass, she's a handful. God bless the poor future bastard who falls in love with her. Especially with Cal being her father. I've already heard him tell her that she's not allowed to even like any boys until she's twenty-one.

"I know. Speaking about trouble, why all the questions about Isla?" Cal's handsome face turns serious, his eyes demanding a response.

"Isla and I are childhood friends, so naturally I'm going to be concerned about her whereabouts."

"I just find it interesting that after two months of being here, you're finally showing some interest in her. Funny how that is coming about after the peep show my son gifted you of her left appendage." I snort out in laughter at Cal's high-end vocabulary for boob.

"Your son is now my favorite out of your two children. I commend you for teaching him young about the appreciation we must show to women's appendages by not covering them up," I joke, her glorious breast still flashing across my mind. "In fact, I'm going to text Robert to find out where they are in order to save her from his encouragement to have sex with a stranger." I take out my phone and text him.

"If there's anyone she needs saving from, it's you." I look up at Cal to see if he's joking, only to find him dead serious. "Please Sean, stay away from her. Jenna likes her and the kids adore her. I don't need her quitting on us just because she feels uncomfortable around you." He rakes his hand through his hair and sighs. "Not to mention, Jenna will hate you."

"Jenna might already be starting to hate me." I look down when my phone buzzes with a text back from Robert. They're at O'Malley's, an Irish bar that used to be Jenna and Robert's regular Wednesday night hangout when Jenna was single. I put my phone back in my pocket and stand up to leave, ignoring Cal's warning. "I think I may be wearing out my welcome. I promise I'm only staying until we leave for the press tour."

"If you told us you wanted to move in, Jenna would be the first one contacting an architect to build you your own guest house," he says wearily, standing up as well. "She loves you like a brother. We both do." He comes around the table and gives me a hard brotherly slap on the back. "I'm happy to see you wanting to get out. You acting like a hermit these last couple of months has been unsettling."

"I just needed to re-charge my batteries after this last movie. Don't worry, I'll be fine. I'm moving on with my life and everything is going to be great," I tell him enthusiastically, trying to believe my own bullshit.

"Just as long as you aren't moving on with my nanny, then everything *will* be great." He slaps me harder this time on the back, his warning stinging my shoulder blade. He turns around and heads in the direction of his bedroom. As I watch him leave, I wish I could promise him that I'll stay away from her.

But even if I did promise that, he'd know I would be lying since I've never been known to keep a promise.

Five

Sean

THE CROWD IS loud and vibrant for a Wednesday night at O'Malley's. The two-for-one drink specials and decent cover band belting out hits from the 80's brings out the young, good-looking, working professionals looking to unwind after a tough day at the office.

I wear my baseball cap low over my eyes, hoping I don't get recognized as I make my way through the crowd to the bar. I don't usually walk around with a bodyguard when I'm here in the States and I don't want to have to start. I like my freedom and try to take advantage of it whenever I can. I signal for the bartender, order a Guinness, and scan the crowd while I wait for my drink. When I initially can't spot Isla and Robert from the bar, I start walking around until I notice a group of men surrounding the pool table. I arrive over there just in time to see Isla lean over to take a shot, her breasts playing peekaboo out of her V-neck cut top. I watch as she narrows her eyes in concentration on the pocket she wants the ball to go into. She bites her lower lip as she quickly executes her shot and then celebrates her victory by hugging Robert. They walk over to their opponents to shake hands. One of their opponents holds her hand while leaning in to whisper something in her ear, his words making her laugh.

She's one of the sexiest creatures I have ever seen.

She's also undeniably drunk.

Her smile is looser and her eyes seem unfocused. She runs her hands through her hair, leaving it wild and untamed. She downs her glass of what looks to be some sort of beer and another man quickly hands her a refill. Robert is by her side, playing the dutiful wingman, but even he's getting loud and obnoxious from his alcohol consumption. I glance at my watch to see that it's only nine o'clock at night, making me wonder how long these two have been drinking to already be in this condition.

"Izzy, let's do a shot! I think a buttery nipple would be the perfect shot to start with." Robert laughs at his own innuendo from the events that transpired today while Izzy blushes and smacks him in the chest. Robert is the constant entertainer with his quick one liners. I know he's trustworthy with how much Jenna and Cal rely on him, but I don't think he can handle all the testosterone that has lined up, eyeing their prey that is a drunk, beautiful girl alone with her gay friend. I think it's time to make my presence known.

"I think a shot of water might be a better idea for right now," I announce while maneuvering myself to the front of their audience. I nod my head in acknowledgement to them and stand next to Isla.

"You invited him here?" Isla practically shrieks at Robert in displeasure.

"I sure did and I bet he would love nothing more than to share your buttery nipple." Robert winks at her with an evil grin, his eyes glinting with mischief. I shake my head at him with a chuckle. Cal and Jenna want me to stay far away from Isla, but Robert seems to encourage the opposite. I don't know what's going through that sneaky brain of his, but if the plan includes Isla in my bed tonight, then I'm game. "You take care of her while I get those shots. These men are getting a little restless for her attention." He makes his way through the crowd, leaving me alone with her. I wrap my arm around her waist, hoping the gesture sets the tone loud and clear that she is mine.

"I'm not your territory to mark, Sean." She tries to remove my hand from her waist, but I haul her closer to my chest and grip her hip. My actions make her glare at me, but she stops fighting.

I reward her with a smile. "I'm just trying to keep you safe, Izzy."

"Do *not* call me Izzy! I'm Isla to you!" she growls, her glowing emerald eyes heated with anger, making me wonder if they would glow like that when I make her come.

"Why can't I call you, Izzy? You've always been Izzy to me." I'm taken aback by how upset she is, not understanding why I, who have known her the longest, am not allowed to call her by her nickname anymore.

"When I hear you call me Izzy, it reminds me of when we were young and how terrible you were to me. Let me tell you something, Mister." She pokes her index finger into my chest, making me wince from the surprising pain of it. "I'm a grown woman who will not tolerate being treated like a child from you just because that's all you remember me as. You have no idea who I am!"

"You're right, I don't know who you are anymore," I agree while leaning in to whisper in her ear, hoping she understands my underlying tone. "But I want nothing more than to get to know this beautiful woman named Isla standing before me." My gaze lingers on her lips and then travels back up to her eyes, which are wide in surprise. "I know, let's start all over again." I let go of her, turning around to give her my back for a few seconds before turning back around, my hand extended out for a hand shake.

"Hi, my name is Sean. I come from Ireland and am visiting this great city of Chicago. I like warm apple pie, furry puppies, and long walks on the beach. I noticed your sexy smile and wanted to introduce myself. What's your name?" I inquire with all of the enthusiasm as a cheerleader, my eyes bright and my smile even bigger. I grab her hand without permission and squeeze, not letting go until I get a response.

She tries to keep a straight face, but can't contain the burst of laughter that comes out. I realize that this is the first time I have heard her genuinely laugh in a very long time. It's light, whimsical and it makes my dick harden within seconds. She's about to say something back when the band starts back up again. Her eyes light up in recognition of the song.

"Ooh, I love this song! Let's dance!" Before I can tell her I don't dance, she slips away from me and heads straight for the dance floor. I slowly follow her, enjoying the view of her perfectly round ass swaying to the band playing *Take On Me* by A-Ha. I position myself at the back of her, but give her enough room to continue dancing. Because of the popularity of the song, the dance floor quickly becomes crowded and I'm suddenly pushed from behind. My arm instinctively goes around her to prevent us from falling forward. Her hands grip my forearm and she looks at me over her shoulder, a wicked smile forming on her lips as she purposely grinds her backside against me. I grit my teeth in agony as my erection strains through my pants, wanting to come out and play. She moves her arms upward and wraps them around my neck, forcing my head closer to her. I lower my nose into the crook of her neck and inhale her vanilla citrus scent that tortures my senses. I place my hands on her hips, squeezing them hard while I steer her into place, making sure our hips are in sync together. She turns her head toward me, our lips only inches apart. Her breath smells sweet from the beer she was drinking. Our eyes lock, hers mirroring exactly what I am feeling:

Desire.

Want.

Need.

A small moan escapes her, drawing my attention back to her parted lips. Her tongue darts out to lick them and my brain is screaming at me to kiss her, to take that full bottom lip in between my teeth. I'm about to claim those succulent lips when

I feel something wet splash against my arm.

"Oops, sorry!" Robert laughs while spilling one of the shots on my arm. Isla removes her arms from around my neck and turns toward Robert. I let go of her hips to wipe off my arm, but she beats me to it by brushing her index fingers against the wet spot on my bicep and then sticking her finger in her mouth and sucking on them.

I can feel my dick crying out in blue ball pain.

Isla grabs her shot and hands me mine.

"To friends—with benefits!" Robert cheers. We clink our shot glasses together and down them with one swift gulp. My eyes never waiver from Isla as I watch her throw her head back and drink. The movement causes her to lose her balance and step backwards, bumping into another patron.

"Hey! Watch where you're going, bitch!" The woman turns around in anger, only to have her voice die down as recognition lights her eyes when she sees me. "Oh, my God, you're Sean Lindsey! Can I get a picture with you?"

I agree, hoping this will be the only person who recognizes me. But her friends start to squeal loudly, like a pack of hyenas, and I know our time at O'Malley's is done.

"Time to go, Robert," I command ten minutes later as the flashes from the selfie pictures are starting to blur my vision.

"If you can manage to pull yourself away from your adoring fans, a little help with Isla would be nice." Robert is holding Isla up, that buttery nipple shot taking her into the land of inebriation.

I apologize to the waiting fans who want a photo and stand next to Isla's free side. I grab her arm and steer her and Robert to the entrance. As soon as we open the door, our vision is blinded by the flashing light bulbs of the paparazzi.

"Sean, over here!"

"Sean, who's the girl?"

"Sean, did you and Cora break up?"

The last question seems to snap Isla's head up, her face showing her disgust at the mention of Cora's name. She looks at me and all the lust has vacated her eyes.

Shit, how did they find out so quickly where I was?

"Mates, a little space please so we can get in our car?" They step back enough for me to walk toward a cab and open the door for Isla and Robert to get in. I give the paparazzi one more photo opportunity by waving at them before getting in the taxi.

Robert gives the driver an address that I recognize as Jenna's downtown condo that she still keeps for sentimental purposes since she inherited it from her grandmother. Fortunately, it's only a few blocks away and glancing at Isla, I doubt she's going to make it longer than that before she either passes out or pukes.

"Do you guys do this every Wednesday?" I question, my curiosity peaked if Isla has gone home with anyone in the past during her escapades with Robert.

"Going to O'Malley's? No. Most of the time we go to dinner, shopping or to the movies. We haven't been to O'Malley's in a long time." His answer makes me feel better knowing that Isla hasn't been with another man for at least as long as I've been in town and possibly longer.

"Does Jenna know that you use her condo on Wednesdays?"

"We don't usually use it, but I didn't think it was a good idea for Isla to return home in this kind of condition." I nod in agreement because Jenna really would hate me if I brought her nanny back drunk.

We arrive at the entrance to Jenna's condo five minutes later. I pay the cab driver and help Robert get Isla into the elevator. Once we reach Jenna's floor, we walk Isla to the door. Robert unlocks it with his spare key and Isla immediately runs to the closest bathroom in Avery's old bedroom.

"I will hold her hair back if you find her some clothes," I suggest to Robert while I head into the bathroom to help Isla. She's hugging the toilet and moaning softly. I pull her hair to the side and start to rub her back.

"Alcohol is the devil," she groans and I can't help but chuckle at how pathetic she sounds. Robert comes back in with a t-shirt, glass of water and two aspirins. Isla cooperates by taking the medicine and drinking the water. She then brushes her teeth with the extra toothbrush that Robert found. She stumbles back into the bedroom and falls flat onto the bed. I start taking off her shoes and socks, studying her feet as I do. I'm not surprised to find that even her feet are pretty. Once her feet are bare, I manage to roll her onto her back and reach for the button on her jeans to take them off so she can be more comfortable.

"I can handle it from here, Sean," Robert interrupts, placing his hand on my forearm to stop me.

"It's quicker if both of us help." I reach for the top of her pants when he stops me again.

"I think it's inappropriate for you to undress her, Sean."

"You think I would take advantage of her while she's passed out? That's insulting, Robert." I stand up in disbelief that he thinks so low of me. "Interesting coming from someone who toasts to friends with benefits." I walk out of the room and into the kitchen to get a glass of water, hoping the coldness of it will cool off my anger. He comes out of the bedroom two minutes later and closes the door.

"I was all for you two hooking up until the paparazzi reminded me that you're still in love with the Wicked Witch of the East." He pours himself a glass of water and downs it.

"I'm not in love with Cora anymore," I growl, tired of people telling me what my feelings are. He looks at me skeptically and I throw my hands up in frustration. "It's hard to turn off years and years of feelings for someone, Robert. I'm working on it."

"I wish you luck, my friend, because you have your work cut out for you in convincing us otherwise." He bids me good night and heads back into the room where Isla is sleeping.

I refill my glass of water and take it with me to the master bedroom. I ponder Robert's words while brushing my teeth with a spare toothbrush when my phone beeps. I look down to see it is a text from none other than Cora herself.

Cora: "Looking forward to seeing you on Friday. XOXO"

I groan out in frustration as I spit the toothpaste out of my mouth and rinse. I don't bother responding back, instead I delete the message.

As I head to bed, I realize that Robert might be right. I do have my work cut out for me and the first person who I need to convince is Isla.

I SIP ON my second glass of red wine and study the photos that I received via email. I tap my fingernails against the table, my mind racing at the scene unfolding.

Sean, Robert, and Isla walking out of a bar together.

Sean and Robert holding onto Isla.

Sean helping Isla into the taxi cab.

Why is Sean going to a very public bar with Jenna's assistant and nanny?

Sure, the nanny isn't just anyone. It's that annoying little twit, Isla, whose childhood crush on Sean was so painfully obvious, it was pathetic. I used to tease him all the time about it whenever I would go home with him for the holidays. He always seemed indifferent. Now he's hanging out with her?

Something doesn't feel right about this.

I grab my secondary cell phone—the one I use to stay anonymous with an unknown number—and call my spy.

Danny Salari's reputation for being an aggressive paparazzi isn't exaggerated. He has aligned himself with people in every single occupation, ranging from garbage men to mailmen, in order to obtain stories on famous people that will create a scandal. A scandal big enough to make millions. I've been paying him for the past three years now to follow Jenna and Cal, more specifically, scaring Jenna into possibly leaving Cal. The man has orchestrated the delivery of graphic death threats of her and their daughter. He even hired someone to run her off the road while she was jogging one day when she lived downtown.

She was fine, unfortunately.

Now that Cal has moved them into a gated community in the suburbs, it has been harder for Danny to do his job. Not to mention his screw up of getting too aggressive with Jenna that resulted in a restraining order placed against him. Because of this, he pays other people to do his dirty work for me, which makes me very nervous. He assures me that my identity is kept confidential, but then again, how do I know he's trustworthy when he's a lying piece of scum who will do *anything* in order to get a story? I've paid that man close to a million dollars to make Jenna's life a living hell and I'm definitely *not* getting a return on my investment.

"Why is Sean out with the nanny and the assistant?" I bark out at him as soon as he picks up the phone. We're well past the stage of formalities in this business relationship, so I'm beyond the point of being nice to him. I have plenty of dirt on Danny in case he ever decides to talk about our little arrangement.

"How the hell should I know? Isn't he your lap dog?" He sneers and sometimes I wonder why I even bother putting up with him. "All I know is that Wednesdays are the nanny's night off and she hangs out with the assistant."

"Is this the first time you've seen Sean out with Isla?" I inquire, wondering if I've missed any other outings between the two of them.

"Yes, it is."

"I want you to start following Sean while he's in Chicago. Since he doesn't have a restraining order against you, I want you to personally be doing it."

"It's going to cost you for me to personally be watching him. There are much bigger stories than Sean Lindsey out there right now that I'm trying to chase." I had a feeling that my luck of not owing him more money was going to run out.

"How much, Danny?"

He's silent for a moment and I can hear the wheels turning as to how much he thinks he should charge me. "One hundred thousand dollars," he finally responds back with.

"Are you mad? 100K for you to sit on your fat ass and take photos of him?" I scream, not even knowing if I even have that kind of money left in my bank account.

"You're asking me to give up going after bigger stories. My time is precious, Cora, and I've been wasting too much of it on your sick obsession. 100K or no following Sean Lindsey."

I squeeze my eyes shut, contemplating what I should do. My cash flow is running out and since I don't have any future movies locked down, I'm hesitant to agree to this deal. I just received my last film paycheck and after I pay every single person who works for me—which is my agent all the way down to my housekeepers—that barely leaves anything left. Not to mention my ridiculously lavish lifestyle that I can't seem to give up.

But with my relationship with Cal being almost non-existent, I feel following Sean is one of the only options left in planning on how to win Cal back. Sean is the only person I still have access to in Cal's inner circle.

"Fine!" I groan, hating the sound of his disgusting joker-like, victory laugh. My stomach actually starts to hurt knowing that this piece of shit has the upper hand right now.

"Half is due tomorrow. You have my bank information," he reminds me and he will definitely not start unless he gets his money.

"I sure fucking do," I mumble, grabbing my computer to log onto my bank account to set up a wire transfer to him.

"Why do you want him followed so badly anyway? Jealous of his new interest in your doppelgänger?" The reference of Isla and I looking alike has always made me livid. We look nothing alike. She may be pretty, but she's no competition for me.

"It's none of your goddamn business why I want him

followed." The less information I can give Danny of my motives, the better if he ever decides to go rogue.

"I hope you truly feel it's worth it, Princess. Chat with you tomorrow." He hangs up and I throw my phone down on the table in aggravation.

After I finish transferring the money, I can't help but go back and study those photos one more time. Sean is my last connection to Cal. I must keep him interested in me, even if that means having sex with him. Not that that would be so bad since Sean is very handsome. He might even be able to make me come for once.

But he is no Cal.

Sean has to stay in love with me, which leaves no room for him to be distracted by the likes of Isla Jones. It's time to start paying more attention to Mr. Lindsey.

And if she ends up being added to the list of collateral damage, so be it.

Seven

Isla

I THINK I can count on one hand how many times I've been hungover in my life and every morning after the night of indulgence, I vow never to drink again.

This morning is no different.

My eyelids feel unbelievably heavy, like they are weighted down. They want to open, but every time they do, a merciless sunbeam shoots straight into my retina, making the ache behind my brow intensify. My tongue is heavy and coated with last night's remnants of toothpaste. It isn't the enticing scent of coffee that has me getting up, but the raunchy smell of throw up coming from my hair. I slowly ease my body out of bed and make my way to the bathroom. I relieve my bladder and decide to take a nice, long hot shower. The steam of the shower helps clear my brain fog and memories from last night start streaming in.

The feeling of how good Sean's hands felt on my hips.

The feeling of how wet my panties got when Sean's hard erection pressed against my backside.

The feeling of electric tingles shooting down my spine with the deliciousness of his breath on my neck.

The overwhelming feeling of need to have his lips on mine.

I ignore the urge to play with myself when my hands wash

over my core and the rest of my body. Instead, I focus on the fact that I need to ignore these feelings for him. Sean Lindsey is a dangerous distraction that I don't need in my life right now. Who am I kidding to think that I could have an emotionless liaison with him? One touch from him would lead to complete heartbreak. What if I do get together with Sean and it goes horribly wrong? I can't afford to lose this job right now. It came into my life at the perfect time and is a stepping stone to my future career of one day opening up my own school.

Or so I thought.

Lately, I've been wavering on if that's really what I want to do with my life, which leads me to question what would I do if I don't pursue what I thought was my dream.

Don't worry about this now, Izzy.

I give my head a good shake and rinse the conditioner out of my hair while giving myself a mental pep talk. *Focus on today and don't worry about tomorrow.* And today I need to focus on being the best role model and teacher I can be to the children.

Speaking of Avery and Brooks…

I turn off the shower and grab a towel since I realize I haven't looked to see what time it is yet. Even though I get Wednesday nights off, I'm usually back at their house and in my own bed in order to be up and ready by eight a.m., which is when the kids get up in the morning. There has only been one other time I have slept out on a Wednesday night and that was at Robert's apartment, but he had me back at the house in plenty of time the following morning because he occasionally works out of Jenna's house.

You don't usually have a set start and end time when you're a live-in caretaker. I just make sure I'm always around for whenever I'm needed. Most of the time I don't even see the children in the morning until I join them for breakfast. Jenna is a very hands-on mother, always getting the children up, dressed and having most, if not all, meals with them. The only time I'm really alone with the kids, outside of homeschooling them, is if she's working or her and Cal decide to go out of town without them. That has only happened a handful of times.

Dread starts to seep into my chest as I recall the sunlight blinding me this morning, leading me to think it might be getting closer to eight in the morning than I thought it would be. I walk into the room, grab my phone, and scream as the screen says it's nine o'clock in the morning.

Fuck, fuck, fuckity, fuck!

"Wake up, wake up!" I start yelling and I throw open the bedroom door and run into the living room, only to come to a screeching halt at the sight of Robert and Sean. Sean is standing in the kitchen, drinking a cup of coffee, while Robert is sitting on the other side of him, slathering cream cheese on his bagel. Both men have a bemused, perplexed look on their faces at my commotion.

"What are you both doing? We've got to get going! I'm going to get fired for being late!"

"Is that the outfit you chose to take care of the children in today? I can guarantee Brooks will show off both of your lady bits dressed in that." Robert nods to the towel wrapped underneath my arms before taking a bite out of his breakfast.

I grip the towel tighter, becoming completely self-conscious about being nude underneath it. Sean's intense stare on my body jumbles my thought process even more. "Of course I'm not going out like this! How long have you two been up and why didn't you wake me sooner?"

Sean comes out of the kitchen, holding an extra cup of coffee for me. I grab it with my free hand and immediately take a sip, sighing in pleasure as the caffeine hits my taste buds. He gives me a sexy smirk at my reaction, which causes me scowl at him, not liking how hot he still looks in his clothes from last night. The man looks fresh as a daisy, whereas I'm struggling to keep my wits about me.

"Here are your clothes from last night, washed and dried." He scoops up my folded clothes that were on the counter and walks them into the bedroom for me since my hands are full at the moment. He comes back out, takes a bagel out of the bag, and places it on a plate for me. "Stop worrying about getting fired. Jenna knows you're with us. All she cared about was that you were safe."

"Jenna knows you're with me? Ugh!" I moan in exasperation, not wanting to be the recipient of a lecture I know is now in my future from her. Jenna knows all about my childhood crush on Sean, courtesy of his big mouth. She has already warned me once not to waste my time on him because of Cora's toxic hold on his heart. I can only imagine what she's possibly thinking now.

"I wasn't going to lie to her. Besides, where else do you think she thought I was if not with you guys?"

"Probably out hooking up with whores," I mutter while turning my back on them, walking into the bedroom, and slamming the door shut. I grab my clothes off the bed and retreat into the bathroom, locking the door since it would be just like him to come after me and open the door without knocking. I quickly get dressed and comb my fingers through my hair, not bothering to try to find a blow dryer to dry it with. I check myself in the mirror, sighing at how terrible I look with red eyes and purple bags underneath them. I take a deep breath, praying that I can score a nap with Brooks today, and go back out to eat my breakfast.

"Where did he go?" I ask in between bites of my bagel when I notice Sean is not there.

"He went to go get his car from O'Malley's so we don't have to walk," Robert answers while looking at his email. I choose to ignore my heart screaming *how nice that is* and force myself to think of anything but Sean and of what transpired last night. Robert and I were having a good time before his appearance and I feel bad the night had to end the way it did.

"Thank you for taking care of me last night and for washing my clothes. That shot really did a number on my stomach." I wince as I recall some of my time praying to the porcelain God.

"I wouldn't touch your nasty upchucked soaked clothes. I love you, but I don't love you that much." My eyes go wide as the realization hits me that Sean was the one who took care of me last night, not Robert.

"Sean took off my clothes?" I whisper in horror, embarrassment starting to stain my cheeks crimson.

"No, I wouldn't let him do that. I removed your clothes and put one of Jenna's old t-shirts on you. Not that he didn't try at first, but I told him it wouldn't be appropriate for him to do so. The only thing he took off of you were your socks and shoes."

"Great, so now I have to thank him." Showing Sean any kind of gratitude is the last thing I want to do right now, but it's the right thing to do since he could have decided to stay at the bar himself instead of coming back with Robert to help.

Damn him for being nice to me! Why couldn't he have met someone else last night to take home?

Robert watches me, a weary smile forming on his lips. "He was genuinely concerned about you last night, so yes, you owe him a thank you." He stands up from the bar stool and starts to clean up.

I finish my bagel and decide to help by making the beds and cleaning any mess that we created. I want to make sure this place looks exactly how it was when we arrived last night to avoid any further trouble with Jenna. She lets her best friend, Layla, and her fiancé, Chase, live in her condo when they come to town for long periods of time, so they would definitely report if the place was a mess.

"Sean is downstairs waiting for us," Robert announces five minutes later. I nod in acknowledgement and grab my purse. We do one more walk through of the condo to see if anything got left behind and then we lock up and leave.

"Thank you again for another fun night off." I break our compatible silence while the elevator descends to the main floor. I give Robert a hug as I truly appreciate him taking me under his wing and becoming my friend. Chicago would be very lonely if I didn't have someone like him.

"It's always fun being your wingman." He winks at me before we step off the elevator. "But Izzy, I was watching how Sean was looking at you. Be warned, that man has his sights set on you." Robert's serious tone is a far cry from his usually light and flirty one, which leads me to believe he doesn't think me being involved with Sean is a good idea.

"Thanks for the warning, but I can take care of myself," I reassure him … or am I trying to reassure myself? "My guard is up with Sean and my relationship with Cal and Jenna is way too important for me to jeopardize. Don't worry, my panties will forever stay intact on my body when Sean Lindsey's around." I joke to Robert since he's always saying that Sean is the master of disintegrating women's panties with his smile.

He throws his head back and barks out a disbelieving laugh. "Oh honey, somehow I doubt that. You have no idea what type of man you're up against." He walks ahead of me to open the passenger door. Sean's handsome face comes into view, looking like a rugged model in his sunglasses with that megawatt, sexy, signature smile of his directed at me.

And just like that, he has deteriorated my confidence *and* my panties.

Eight

Sean

I REALLY WANTED to talk to Isla about last night, but the day provided little opportunity for alone time with her. As soon as we returned, Jenna whisked her and the kids away, but not before giving me her stink eye of disapproval. Cal was downtown for meetings and Robert was working from the main office, so I spent the day by myself. I thought I was going to be bored, but I shocked myself by acting like an adult and being productive. I not only worked out in their home gym, but answered emails, read some scripts for potential movies, and even made myself my own lunch, which sad to say, I haven't done in a very long time. After an afternoon jerk off session, I decided to continue reading scripts while waiting for everyone to return home for dinner when the next thing I know, I'm waking up to a pitched dark bedroom. I blindly grope for my phone on the night stand to discover that it's nine o'clock at night.

How the hell have I slept for five hours?

I know I didn't get much sleep last night, tossing and turning over my concern for the condition Isla was in. But I can't remember the last time I ever took a nap, much less one so long.

My stomach starts growling, reminding me that I haven't eaten dinner, so I decide to go downstairs to see if anyone is home and to raid the refrigerator.

The house is silent as I make my way downstairs, which doesn't surprise me since it's past the kids' bedtime. I check out the movie room to see if Cal and Jenna are watching a movie, but it's empty. I refuse to go walking by their room, not wanting to hear any sexual animalistic noises coming from behind their closed door. I head toward the kitchen, wondering if anyone noticed my absence at all when a note on the refrigerator door grabs my attention:

Dinner inside, Sleeping Beauty!
Love, J

I can't help the goofy smile that comes across my face. Jenna has a heart of gold and even though she was pissed at me earlier, she'll forever watch over me as if she's one of my blood sisters.

Cal's one lucky bastard, but I knew she was a diamond in the rough the first moment I met her.

Now it's my turn to find my own.

I take the leftovers out of the refrigerator and open the container. Doubt starts to creep in as I see their chef has attempted to make shepherd's pie. The only shepherd's pie I will eat is my Nana's when I'm home in Ireland. Anyone else who isn't from the motherland tempting to make it is rubbish.

But, it's late and I'm ravenous. So I place it in a bowl and warm it up in the microwave. I pour myself a nice, cold Guinness to go with it since I can only imagine how bland it's going to taste. The microwave dings and I take out what now looks like mush. I grab a fork, take a big swig of my drink first, and decide to dive into my food.

It's one of the most delicious shepherd's pie I've ever had.

"Huh," I wonder out loud to no one, impressed that Cal and Jenna's chef knows how to make traditional shepherd's pie. I finish it in five big bites, drink the rest of my beer, wash my dishes, and put them in the dishwasher. I get ready to turn off the lights to the kitchen when something outside of the window catches my attention. I walk toward the window to get a closer look to find someone swimming laps in the pool.

That someone being Isla and then it dawns on me.

Isla probably made that shepherd's pie.

Jenna has mentioned before that Isla has cooked some traditional Irish dishes for them.

Damn, she's hot, smart, and can cook?

Wanting confirmation, I walk to the patio doors to go visit her. This would also be the perfect time to discuss what transpired between us since I'm ready for a repeat performance.

I stop at the ledge of the stairs and watch her swim toward me. She's swimming in the breast stroke position, so I know she can see that she has company. As she gets closer to the stairs, she goes under the water and swims underneath until her hand touches the stairs. She loudly inhales for air as she breaks free from the surface of the water.

"Did you make that shepherd's pie?"

"Why do you want to know?" she asks while pushing her hair that is clinging to her face behind her ears.

"It was one of the best damn pies I've ever eaten." I look her in the eyes and compliment her with sincerity.

"You're welcome. Now what are you doing out here?"

"I wanted to watch you swim." I raise my eyebrow at her, giving her a teasing smile.

"Well, don't. It's creepy." Before I can even respond, she dives back into the pool and starts swimming toward the deep end. I watch, admiring her firm ass bob in and out of the pool as she reaches the end and swiftly turns back around to come back. Her being alone in the pool gives her the upper hand at ignoring me, so I decide to take matters into my own hands.

I start taking off my clothes and by the time she comes up for air in the shallow end, I'm down to my skivvies and a wicked smile.

"Wh…what the hell are you doing?" she stammers in between coughs as she accidentally swallows water due to her mouth being open in shock from the sight of me.

"Joining you for a swim."

I slowly walk into the pool, not taking my eyes off her the whole time. She's wearing a one-piece bathing suit that does nothing to hide the sexy curves of her body.

"But you aren't in a bathing suit?" Her eyes are wide with shock since I'm now completely submerged in and only a few feet away from her.

"That has never stopped me before." I inch closer to her, watching her eyes light up with desire as she looks up and down my body. I see her gulp when I stop directly in front of her. "I think we need to discuss last night."

Her head snaps up to attention, her eyes now focused on mine. "I don't remember last night."

"I remember last night perfectly." My eyes look down as she parts her lips and I slowly move past her to stand directly in back of her. "Let me refresh your memory," I whisper seductively into her ear.

She looks at me over her shoulder as I wrap my arms around her waist. She gasps when I bring her hard against my chest, her ass settling perfectly against my growing erection. I nudge my nose into the same spot from last night and exhale the breath I was holding, hoping she smelled as good as I remembered.

She smells even fucking better.

I rub my nose up her neck, causing her to shiver from desire. She wraps her arms around my forearms and leans her head back to give me better access. My lips brush against her ear lobe and she moans out in pleasure when I gently graze my teeth against the delicate skin.

"Do you know I thought about you today? I remembered how your enticing scent drove my senses crazy. I remembered how perfect you fit in my arms last night while we danced. The anticipation of being able to touch you again made me come so hard. When my hand gripped and rubbed down my cock, I imagined what it would feel like being inside of you."

"Sean," she meekly whispers, her voice laced with passion. "We shouldn't be doing this."

Yet she does nothing to push me away.

I spin her around, press her against me and touch my forehead to hers, our breaths becoming one as we breathe hard into one another. Our lips are only inches away from touching. I look deep into her eyes and for the slightest of seconds, I hesitate. I lift my head away from her and search her face for any signs as to why we should stop and run away from each other. Yes, this is my childhood friend, but we're more like two strangers standing here, deeply attracted to one another. Her hands are tightly gripping my biceps, her eyelids are heavy with lust. It's crystal clear that she wants me just as much as I want her, but once this kiss happens, we will forever have crossed that fine line into unknown waters to an undefined relationship. And that is why I hesitate.

I don't want to hurt Izzy.

But I ache with desire for her.

I can't promise a future together.

But I can't imagine not touching her.

I want to take it slow and get to know her.

But I can't wait to be inside of her.

This kiss will change everything between us and as I stare into her eyes, I wonder if she's ready for this.

Because I'm ready to dive right into her.

My eyes zero in on her lush, inviting lips and I slowly make my way toward them, licking my lips in anticipation. I close my eyes, ready for contact when Isla's loud gasp snaps my eyelids open, causing me to shrink away from the blinding outdoor lights that someone has turned on us.

Isla jumps away from me as if I burned her and starts swimming in the opposite direction from me. I shield my eyes from the glaring light, trying to see if a figure can be made out behind the windows inside the house. I turn toward the stairs that lead out of the shallow end. I walk out of the pool and make my way around it to where Isla is climbing up the ladder out of the deep end.

"Meet me in my room," I command softly when I get closer to her, wanting to continue where we left off. She shakes her head no and turns to leave, but not before I reach out, grab her arm, and spin her around.

"I can get fired for this, Sean!" she hisses and snatches her arm out of my grasp.

"No, you won't. I will talk to Cal." I reach again for her, but she side-steps out of my way.

"Cal is not who I'm concerned with." She starts walking toward the cabana bathroom door, making me have to run past her and stop in her path, forcing her to stop to look at me.

"This is going to happen, Isla. Tell me you don't want this and I will back down," I challenge her as I grip her chin, forcing her to look into my eyes. I need her to see how serious I am about this and I do everything I can to convey that in my facial expression. Her emerald eyes show fear and determination, but not rejection. She searches my face briefly before shaking her head out of my grasp.

"I need some space to think, Sean. Give me some time."

"How much time?" I question, making me wonder if she realizes how short our time left with each other really is before I have to leave.

"I don't know—just leave me alone for right now." I don't try to stop her this time as I watch her go inside the house.

I take a deep ragged breath and look around for another towel, only to see that there was only the one that Isla had brought with her. I envy that towel that is wrapped around her tight, warm body. Exactly where I wanted to be tonight. I look down to see my cock still standing for attention.

"Looks like we're going to be taking another cold shower," I mutter while I make my way to the cabana bathroom for some relief.

I will leave Isla alone for now.

Twenty-four hours should be plenty of time.

Nine

Isla

SLEEP EVADES ME as I toss and turn all night long, worry and longing occupying my mind. Worrying about who discovered us in the pool. Longing for Sean, his words, and how he consumes my every thought, which has now created an argument between my head and my heart.

He will only break your heart.

Maybe he won't.

He still loves Cora.

Maybe he really doesn't.

Don't let him touch you.

Give him a chance.

You have nothing to lose.

You have everything to lose.

The question remains, is Sean worth losing it all? My job *and* my heart?

As the sun starts to streak the early morning sky, I give up trying to sleep and get up to start the day. Today's lesson plan for Avery is going to be out of the house so I can avoid Sean and his handsome face. He completely shuts down my defenses and makes it impossible for me to remember why being with him would be a bad idea.

Not expecting anyone to be awake yet, I go downstairs to

make breakfast for everyone as a nice surprise. I enter the kitchen and stop short at the sight of Cal sitting at the island, sipping on a cup of coffee, and reading the newspaper.

"Good morning, Isla." He nods in greeting as he folds his paper and looks at me. I swallow my dread at being under his intense scrutiny. Maybe I won't be making breakfast anymore.

"Good morning, sir. I apologize for disturbing you. I will come back later." I turn on my heel to walk out when he calls out my name, stopping me in my tracks.

"I think we need to have a chat about what I interrupted last night between you and Sean."

Fuck, fuck, fuckity, fuck!

I am so fired!

"I don't know you as well as Jenna does and quite honestly, that was done on purpose. Jenna has been thrust into a world where everyone wants to fill her head with doubt about me and our relationship, so I don't need to add any fuel to the fire that is already out there about how we have a pretty nanny in our employment. There are already disgusting stories in the tabloids that you and I are having an affair or that we're all having threesomes together." I gasp in shock, outrage that people make up such vile, untrue stories. Cal just shrugs at my reaction. "Unfortunately, this comes with the territory of working for us and I'm truly sorry about that."

"Are you letting me go, sir?" I blurt out, my stomach in knots over the agony of having to leave the kids. I honestly don't care that my reputation is being shredded with lies in the public. I'll call my parents to warn them, but they never read the tabloids knowing full well they are filled with rubbish.

"No, we're not letting you go, but Jenna wanted me to talk to you about Sean." I exhale a sigh of relief at his words, despite not liking to hear that Jenna also knows about last night. I blink back the tears that were threatening to spill since crying in front of Cal is the last thing I want to do.

"There's nothing going on between me and Mr. Lindsey,

sir. I can assure you that nothing will happen. This job is very important to me. I love your children and really enjoy working for you and Ms. Pruitt. I give you my word I will stay away from him." I look Cal straight in the eyes, my voice firm with the acknowledgement that I know what the consequences may be if I continue engaging with Sean.

He smiles and shakes his head at me. "You don't understand that once Sean has his sights set on something, he won't let it go until he has no more use for it." He gives me a knowing look and understanding fills my head at his meaning.

"It's nice to see Sean interested in someone else other than Cora and you might be the person who finally rids him free of her. Unfortunately, trying to discover if you are indeed that person might lead to heartbreak. We've been down this road before with him. If you choose to continue a relationship with him, my warning to you is to be careful. As much as I love him like a brother, I'm weary of what his true intentions are with you."

"I promise nothing will happen between us," I reassure him, hoping we can end this discussion so I can run back to my room and hide until the kids are awake.

"Don't make promises you can't keep, Isla." He stands up and pours himself a second cup of coffee. "Consider yourself warned. What you choose to do is your prerogative." He gives me one last smile before heading out of the kitchen.

I walk over to the counter and slowly sit down on the barstool, my hand over my racing heart. This conversation with Cal was scarier than any serious conversation I've ever had with my own father. But, I'm relieved that this happened and quite frankly, I'm happier this conversation comes from Cal and not Jenna. *Will Cal say something to Sean about this?* They have meetings with their agent today downtown, so I wouldn't be surprised if this turns out to be a car ride conversation. Dread starts to fill me, wondering if Sean will back down once Cal talks to him.

Do I want him to stop pursuing me?

Hell no, my heart screams.

It's for the best, my head responds.

I've got to get out of this house. Screw making breakfast, I'm taking the kids out to eat.

I grab my cell phone out of my pocket and text Jenna, asking permission to start our day so I can concentrate on everything else but Sean Lindsey.

"THIS HAS BEEN the best day *ever!*" Avery screams while she skips toward the car for us to make our way back home. Her arms are filled with two stuffed animals that are almost the same size as her. Her aqua eyes are shining with delight, her ponytail barely holding her hair back anymore. I love seeing her like this and I laugh at her excitement, happy that she feels this way since it has been a pretty great day.

As soon as I got the green light from Jenna to take them, I grabbed Brooks' stroller, diaper bag, snacks, and a bodyguard to start our adventure. We ate breakfast at a local restaurant before making the trip to downtown Chicago. We started at the Shedd Aquarium, ate lunch, walked over to the Adler Planetarium, and ended our day at the Lincoln Park Zoo. I'm envious of Brooks right now, who has been sleeping the last hour and stays asleep while I strap him into his car seat. I get into the passenger seat of the car and nod to our bodyguard that we are ready to go. I text Jenna to let her know that we are on our way and then I sit back and try to relax as we ease into Friday evening traffic.

Today was exactly what I needed because I didn't think about Sean while I was with the kids. I feel the situation is cut and dry—either I'm going to be with him or not. I know that he's only staying with us until it's time for the press tour and then who knows where he's going after that. He owns properties in Ireland and London, but barely spends time at either of those places. Sean's a gypsy and is showing no signs of slowing down. He has unlimited funds, endless opportunities, and women throwing themselves at his feet.

And I'm just a nanny.

Helping to shape children's futures is far more important than being an actor, but, unfortunately, we don't get the same respect and pay. Sure, I come from money, but I was taught at a very young age that nothing will be handed to me. That I can go and be whatever I want, but I better work hard at it. So I have. I'm a strong, independent woman who has paved my own life, made my own money, and I'm determined to one day open a school that will be a home to educate young women on how to do the same.

We are worlds apart and nothing is going to change that.

I snap out of my thoughts when I realize we're almost home. I turn around to tell Avery, only to notice that she's fast asleep like her brother. I text Jenna when we pull through the gate to let her know. We pull into the garage just as Jenna opens the door to help get one of the children out. We carry them to their bedrooms and put them in their beds fully clothed, not wanting to take the chance at waking them since they're probably done for the evening.

"Are you hungry? Dinner is ready." I nod at Jenna and follow her to the dining room. She motions for me to sit while she heads toward the kitchen and comes back with our food. I notice only two place settings are prepared and wonder if Cal and Sean are still downtown.

"So tell me how today was? I missed them so much," Jenna says before taking a bite of her salad. I recap our daily activities, telling her how I incorporated my lesson plan with what we saw today. I told her how adorable Avery was when she saw the dolphins and how Brooks slept through the whole planetarium show.

"Sounds like it was a great day! I'm sad I missed it, but so grateful to you for taking them. Thank you, Isla." She wipes her mouth with her napkin and puts it down. "I know Cal talked with you this morning about Sean. I just want to let you know that I'm here if you ever need to talk or anything." She smiles and looks down at her hands, not being able to hide her awkwardness.

I smile back, but don't want to have another conversation of how Sean is wrong for me. "Thank you. Where are Cal and Sean anyway? I thought they would be back by now."

"They decided to stay and have dinner with Philip. They had a lot to go over today before the press tour."

"What are the plans for the press tour? Are we still all going?" I ask, curious as to what our schedule will be since I would like to take some time off to go home and see my parents and friends.

"Everyone will come with us to London. You and the kids will stay with Cal's family while Cal and I go to the Paris and Berlin premiere. We will then spend an extra week back in the UK, which I figured you might want to take off to go home to Ireland or just do whatever you want to do."

I nod in excitement, happy that she was thinking exactly what I was hoping for. "That would be wonderful, Jenna, if I can have that week off and go home."

"Of course you can. You can just meet us in New York for the next premiere and then Cal and I will go by ourselves to the Los Angeles premiere while you stay here with the kids. I'll get the whole itinerary from Robert on paper for you to have." She picks up her phone to send Robert a quick text before she forgets.

"How did today go for you? Is everything settled for the party tomorrow?" I knew taking the kids out of the house would also benefit Jenna, as she had her staff come to do one more walk through of her house for Cal's birthday surprise party. Sean plans on taking Cal out the whole day with sailing and golfing while Jenna's staff and vendors set up the party for outside. Cal is not due back until night time. Jenna will have the curtains inside drawn close so Cal can't see everyone hiding outside and then she will persuade him to come outside for the big surprise.

"Everything seems to be in place. While I'm excited to see his reaction, I'll be happy when this party is over with." I laugh with her and am about to ask more questions when we hear a door slam and footsteps walking toward us. Cal walks in the doorway and smiles. He goes straight to Jenna, looks lovingly into her eyes before kissing her on the mouth.

I glance over my shoulder to see if Sean follows suit, but after ten-seconds and still no Sean, I can't keep my curiosity at bay.

"Where's Sean?" I inquire, looking at Cal. He grimaces and looks down at Jenna before answering me.

"He's with Cora."

Ten

Sean

I SHOULDN'T BE here right now, not with her.

I should've gone to dinner with Cal and Philip instead.

I should've never answered my text messages when I saw them, saying she had landed in Chicago.

But I did answer, and here we are at dinner together.

My appetite is gone with the knowledge that Isla probably now knows where I am and who I'm with. If Cal didn't tell her, then the gossip television news probably did because the paparazzi were waiting for us when we arrived at the restaurant. Out of all the places to eat in Chicago, they just happened to know we were coming here. *I* didn't even know we were coming here until Cora's driver pulled up to the front of the restaurant.

Did she call the paparazzi? I wonder. *And if so, why?* I shake my head at this, refusing to believe she would be that calculated. I continue toying with my food, half listening to a word she is saying. She's complaining about how mean Philip has been to her and that she's thinking of hiring a different agent. I wish she would since that would be another tie severed from her. But she's all talk because I know she won't.

Because keeping Philip is another connection to Cal for her.

Just like I am.

I look up at this realization and study her. She looks beautiful, as usual, but tonight she's very dressed up for a casual dinner. Her dark hair is down in soft waves around her shoulders. Her makeup highlights her sharp cheekbones, her black heavy eye liner bringing out her cat-like eyes. Her white, off shoulder dress shows the smooth silkiness of her shoulders while giving a hint of her cleavage. The dress stops above her knees, showcasing her slender legs and ankles, with her feet looking delicate in bright red heels that match her lipstick. She looks like she's Snow White with how the ambient lighting in the restaurant makes her glow.

A very naughty, evil Snow White.

"Why are you staring at me like that, Sean? Do I have something on my face?" I shake my head and look back down at my uneaten food, disappointment lacing through my veins as I've realized what a waste my night has been.

"Can you show a little bit more enthusiasm for wanting to be here with me, Sean? You're starting to give a girl a complex." She laughs, but it wasn't genuine. I stare into her eyes and see a flash of hurt before her walls are put right back into place.

"Why are we friends, Cora?" I question abruptly, curious as to what her answer may be. I know she would never tell me the real truth as to why she keeps me around, but even her lies would be entertaining to hear.

"What kind of question is that?" She looks genuinely confused and caught off guard by my question. That's exactly how I want her to be. I don't want her to have time to think about what the perfect answer should be.

"A simple one, really. Why are we friends?" I lean back in my seat, cross my arms against my chest, and raise my eyebrows at her. She continues to look at me, but this time with a blank stare. She really is a good actress because I know the wheels are turning in her brain to try to figure out what kind of answer I'm looking for.

"Sean, we've been friends for close to eighteen years. We started our careers together. We have vacationed together. We have been through highs and lows together. You know all about my family, just like I know all about your family. Why wouldn't we be friends?" She challenges back and I mentally give her kudos for trying to turn the question back around on me.

"I know what I bring to our friendship, but what do you bring to our friendship?"

"Excuse me?" Her voice has gained an octave and I can tell she's insulted, but strangely enough, I don't give a fuck. I want to know what she thinks she brings to the friendship. "Have I done something to upset you, Sean?"

"You have done many things that have upset me, Cora. Answer the question."

"I've been a constant companion for you, Sean. I've been there for you when you were lonely, needed a date, or just wanted to hang out. Isn't that what friends do?" She throws down her napkin in disgust and I notice she has barely eaten as well. Come to think of it, Cora has never really been a big eater. "What the hell is wrong with you tonight? This questioning of my friendship with you is quite upsetting." Damn, if I don't see tears start to glimmer in her eyes.

Doubt starts to creep into me, making me question if I'm being too hard on her. She has helped fill that void of loneliness whenever I needed someone around. There were many drunken nights where she took care of me when I needed help. What ulterior motive could she have had to do any of that?

I still want to believe that it was all out of the small goodness of her heart. That I hold some small part of that heart, if anything as a friend.

I sigh and signal the waiter to bring the check. "I'm sorry, Cora. You're right."

"You ruined our dinner tonight, Sean. I was so happy to see you." She shakes her head, takes her napkin, and dabs at her wet eyes.

She deserves a goddamn Academy Award for tonight's performance.

"You're right, I did." I pull out some cash and pay the bill for the food and wine we barely consumed. I stand up and wait for her as she slowly rises out of her seat. With her head held high and a small smile plastered to her face, she gracefully walks out of the restaurant like a gazelle, her body language screaming for people to stop what they're doing and watch her. We wave to the paparazzi while we briskly walk to our awaiting car.

"Back to the hotel," she snaps to the driver while he maneuvers us away from paparazzi that surrounded the car. Silence engulfs us as she turns toward her window, clearly not wanting to speak to me.

I take out my phone to see if I have any text messages and am disappointed that I have none. I decide to text Isla, telling her I will be home shortly and that I would like to talk with her. I need to explain to her that nothing happened tonight with Cora.

"Sean," Cora starts as she turns to me and grabs my wrist while I'm holding my phone. "I forgive you for tonight. I think we need to start fresh and forget about our conversation at dinner. Why don't you come up to my room for a drink and we can talk?" She gives me a seductive smile that for once does not seem to work on me.

"I'm tired, Cora. It has been a long day and tomorrow will be another one as well. I think we should just call it a night." I check my phone to see if Isla has responded. Her lack of response makes me eager to get back home.

The car pulls in the front of the hotel. I go to grab the handle of my door, when Cora's hand stops me.

"I'm sorry you aren't your normal self tonight, Sean. Why doesn't my driver take you back home?" She nods at the driver, who's watching her from the rearview mirror.

"Are you cool with that, mate?" I ask when I catch his gaze in the mirror. It would be nice not to have to find another ride home.

"Yes, sir," he answers before exiting the car to open Cora's door.

"Feel better, Sean, and I look forward to seeing you tomorrow night." She leans in and gives me a hug, but before I can pull away, she plants a kiss on my lips that lingers longer than normal. Shocked by the touch of her lips, I wait to feel my dick stir, but nothing happens. She pulls back, caresses my cheek with her hand, and exits the car.

I give the driver the address to Cal and Jenna's house and as I do, I notice that he looks slightly familiar. I stare at him a moment longer, trying to recall where I've seen him before. His hat is pulled down low, almost to the point where I can't see his eyes.

"Do you work full-time for Cora as her driver?" Not being able to remember where I've seen him before is driving me crazy. Is Cora doing that well that she can afford a full-time driver?

"No, sir. This is my first time driving Miss Gregory." He doesn't even look at me when he responds. I give up trying to remember since it doesn't matter and look at my phone to see if Isla has texted me back. When I see she hasn't, I continue to send her a string of text messages.

Me: Almost home and we really need to talk.

Me: Isla, are you awake? Please answer me if you are.

Me: Dinner was innocent, I swear! Just two friends having a casual meal.

Me: Please don't be mad at me, Isla. I swear on the Harrington children, who you know I love as if they were my own, that NOTHING HAPPENED with Cora tonight. You've got to believe me.

Me: Please talk to me, Isla!

Twenty minutes go by and she still hasn't responded. I put my phone back in my pocket, giving up on sending her anymore text messages. My reaction to Cora tonight leads me to believe that I *am* over my romantic feelings for her and I do think it is all because of Isla. I can have with Isla what Cora refuses to ever give me.

Isla is warmth and light, whereas Cora is cold and dark.

I was so used to being around Cora's dark, magnetic pull, that I didn't know what it felt like to want someone who is like Isla.

Someone who is selfless, puts other people's needs before their own, who is sweet and genuinely kind. Unfortunately, I can't say the same thing for Cora.

Now that I have gotten a taste of what I can possibly have with Isla, why would I ever go back to wanting the polar opposite with Cora?

My thoughts are interrupted as we pull up to the security guardhouse. The driver announces me, but I pull down my window instead so the guard can physically see that it's me and hand him my license. He hands it back and opens the gate for us to pull forward. We get to Jenna and Cal's gate, where I proceed to jump out of the car and press the code in so the driver doesn't know it. I have no clue as to what kind of reputation this driver has and I'm not taking any chances with him having their code. I get back in the car while the gate opens and he drives us through.

"Thank you for bringing me home. I know it was not part of the original itinerary." I hand him a large tip and look him up and down one last time as the nagging feeling that I know him from somewhere still has not left me. He says thank you, gets back into his car before I can ask for his card, and drives off. I remind myself to ask Cora tomorrow why he looks so familiar. Maybe she can shed some light on the mystery.

The house is quiet and dark when I let myself in, indicating that everyone is asleep. I look at my watch to see that it is almost eleven at night. I still don't have any text messages back from Isla. Because of that, I go straight to her room.

I quietly tiptoe along the carpet. I listen outside of her door for the television, but I hear nothing. I grab the doorknob and slowly try to turn it, only to find that it won't budge.

She locked her door.

What a clever girl.

With a smile on my lips, I take out my phone and proceed to

type out another text message to her while walking to my room.

Me: *I see you have locked your door tonight. Well played, m'lady! But a locked door will not deter me, Izzy. I hope you have sweet dreams filled with me in them.*

I finish the text and sigh in contentment, already feeling better being under the same roof as her.

Eleven

Cora

As SOON AS I get into my hotel room, I text Danny, demanding that he call me back ASAP. Sean was so distant tonight and I felt my grip on him slowly slipping away from me. If I lose Sean, then Cal is gone to me forever. I need to up my game with Sean. I quickly send him a text, hoping he's not spending time with that bitch, Isla.

Me: I can still taste you on my lips and I crave more. Until tomorrow ... I know my dreams will be filled with you. XOXO

I roll my eyes while texting this utter nonsense. Men are such visual creatures and it's so easy to stimulate their brains via text messaging. *Maybe I should send him a seductive selfie?* I've never had to before, but I hear they're quite effective. I ponder this when my phone vibrates in my hand and I see Danny is calling me back.

"Tell me you were able to get the code to their gate?" I start pacing back and forth, hoping that having Danny drive Sean home tonight was a success. I had it planned that Danny was going to act as my chauffeur in hopes that I could lure Cal or Sean into spilling some information for Danny to hear and use. Danny rented an SUV and dressed the part, even getting a hat and growing out a beard to help disguise his identity.

"No, he was smart enough to jump out of the car and enter

it himself. He completely blocked my view from seeing the numbers. I think he recognized me, Cora. Not directly, but he kept staring at me as if I looked familiar to him. If can recognize me even with this disguise, then I can't be anywhere near Cal Harrington."

"Agh!" I huff out in frustration. "Fine, pay one of your other friends to be my driver. Have them set up a camera and video in the car." If I can get Sean in the car with me again and seduce him, it will make one helluva a story and get little Miss Isla to stop being a distraction.

"It's safer this way, Cora. That way they can also hide and try to take photos of the party without getting recognized as well. What time do they need to pick you up?"

"The party officially starts at seven o'clock, but I want to make an early appearance. Have them be downstairs at my hotel at six thirty. They better not be late and they better be dressed for the part, Danny." I hang up on him before he can respond.

I pour myself a glass of wine and take a big gulp, hoping the alcohol will start to calm my nerves. I take the glass over to my closet and look in satisfaction at the dress I bought for tomorrow. *If you even want to call it a dress.* It shows everything, leaving little to the imagination. The perfect dress to have everyone's attention focused on me.

Jenna will be an afterthought once I show up to Cal's party.

Twelve

Sean

I WAS GIVEN strict instructions by Jenna to keep Cal away from the house so they can prepare for his surprise party. I arranged for a round of golf, lunch, and sailing on Lake Michigan under the pretense that it was Philip demanding a boy's day of fun while he was in town. Cal would have no problem turning me down, but he wouldn't turn Philip down. Fortunately, the weather cooperated for all of our outdoor excursions and we had a fun day.

We drop Philip off at his hotel and I notice that it isn't even six o'clock yet. Jenna didn't want me to bring Cal home until seven. I scramble to think of how I can keep him occupied for one more hour but nothing sounds convincing.

"Let's get something to eat. I'm starving! Where's a good hot dog joint so I can try one of these famous Chicago dogs?"

He looks at me with an amused smile and gives the driver a name of a restaurant to go to. "Will this just be a snack, because I'm sure there will be plenty of food at the party?"

Shit, how does he know?

I decide it's best to play dumb since he might be trying to trick me into revealing details. "What are you talking about? What party?"

"For the safety of my family, I'm told who comes in and out

of my household at any moment by the guards at the gatehouse and the private security I hire to sit outside of my house all day long. Naturally, I put two and two together with the number of vendors that have been arriving today."

"You still spy on Jenna?" I ask incredulously. "How do you even get away with that without her being mad at you?"

"Jenna has learned that everything I do is for her and the children's best interest. She trusts me completely and since she has nothing to hide from me, she isn't bothered by it. Half the time I think she even forgets since she doesn't see where the security is positioned. We still get the occasional death threat, so she's more than willing to let me take whatever steps I deem necessary to keep our family safe."

"Wow." I'm stunned speechless at the measures Cal takes for their safety. "Can you at least act surprised so Jenna doesn't think I told you?"

"Of course I can. I'm told I'm a pretty decent actor," he jokes, playing down the fact that he's won an Academy Award already. "What time did she say we had to be back?"

"She wants us back at seven. I must warn you that I invited Cora by accident. So do me a favor and please ignore her, because I promised Jenna I would keep her away from her and the kids. Since you barely ever leave Jenna's side, can you make sure you mingle with your guests without Jenna for a little bit?" I plead, really not wanting Cora to cause any scenes, because I know she will if she doesn't get any attention from Cal.

"No, I don't think so. Why should I deprive myself of my fiancée's company in order to satisfy Cora?"

"Cal, you sound like one of those pathetic men who are pussy-whipped by their woman. Don't be one of those blokes," I joke, but my smile quickly fades as I see anger radiating out of Cal's eyes.

"Jenna and our children are the best thing that has ever happened to me. They make me want to be a better man. They push me to be that better person, which only makes me a better actor and director. My life doesn't function without Jenna. She's my partner, my soulmate." He stares out of the window while he continues to talk. "Life is precious, Sean. She can be taken away from me in a blink of an eye. I don't want to be without her for even a second out of the day."

"Okay, Cal, I'll think of some other way to keep Cora at bay." I shove my hand through my hair, wishing I never opened my big mouth in the first place to hear his lovey-dovey speech.

He shakes his head, his tone laced in disappointment. "You don't take me seriously, because you can't understand what this feeling is. You won't ever understand with someone like Cora. She'll never be a true and equal partner to you. She'll never treat you the way you deserve to be treated. I wish you'd open your eyes and start seeing that."

"I am starting to see that, Cal. After all these years, she still wants you. It has always been you!" I can't hide my disgust at knowing I've always been second best in Cora's eyes. We've actually never talked about Cora and how she feels about him, or me.

"I've never given her any reason for it to be me, Sean. There was only that one incident in the bathroom years ago that you thankfully interrupted. I don't even know how we got into that bathroom, because she kept refilling my drinks to the point where I was ready to pass out. Other than that, I have always just tried to be a big brother to her. You must know that, Sean." I stare at him in silence, not ready to respond. "Did you ever doubt my loyalty to you? Did you really believe I would be with her knowing how you felt about her?"

"No, I never doubted your loyalty, Cal," I sigh, tired of the topic of Cora and how she's wrong for me. I finally *know* she's wrong for me, but no one seems to believe me.

"Do you want what I have, Sean? Do you want to have a soulmate in your life?" He questions, staring into my eyes to see if I'll tell the truth or lie to him.

"Of course I do, Cal," I quietly confirm since I do want what he has. I'm green with envy with what he has with Jenna and I know I'll never get that from Cora. Even if she did want me, she's too selfish of a person. She would demand that I treat her like a Queen, but never give the same respect back to me. It would never be an equal partnership with her.

"Then let Cora go. Forever. Cut all ties from her and wish her adieu." At first, I think he's joking, but there's no playfulness or jesting in his stern facial expression. His aqua eyes are cold and emotionless.

"Don't you think that's a little harsh, Cal? We've been friends since we were fifteen years old. You know how horrible her mother is, how hard her childhood was. What good would it do for her if we sever all ties from her?"

"That's just it, Sean, it shouldn't be just about her, but about all of us. About you! What does she bring to the table as your friend? A buddy when you're lonely? She craves attention and demands she gets it. She isn't even a nice person—not to you, not to me, not to anyone. She should be happy for me that I have found someone who loves me unconditionally for me and not for my fame and fortune, yet she disrespects Jenna every time she sees her. I can't have that toxicity in my life. After this press tour for our movie, I'm done with Cora and you should consider doing the same, especially if you want to have a serious relationship with anyone else."

I know he's right, but the thought of cutting Cora completely out of my life is hard to swallow. I know she's wrong for me, but that doesn't mean I want to hurt her by ostracizing her. Fortunately, I don't have to make this decision tonight since the focus of the evening is all on Cal.

"What are your intentions with Isla?" Cal demands, bringing up another topic of conversation that I prefer not to have. Isla never responded to my texts and she refused to look at me this morning while at breakfast.

"Honestly, I don't know. I just know that I'm having a hard time staying away from her. I think about her the moment I wake up until the moment I go to sleep. We haven't had sex yet, but it's imminent." I glance over at him and see his jaw tense up.

"Any chance I can convince you that this is a bad idea? That you need to think of her heart that you're going to break? How awkward it will be for her to see you after you have your way with her and then leave her?"

I wince at the harshness of his words. "I don't plan on loving and leaving her, Cal."

"Really? Then what are your plans? Marrying her? Of course not," he responds when I don't answer him right away. The car stops in front of a famous Chicago hot dog restaurant, exactly what I was wanting before this conversation started.

"Cal, I'm just trying to understand these new found feelings for her. Cora is the only other person I have felt this way about. Trust me, I understand the repercussions and I'm trying to figure out a solution on how nobody gets hurt."

"That's not life, Sean. Someone is going to get hurt and my bet is it will be Isla. And you will be the one who has to live with that on your conscience. If you even have one." He pushes open the door and slams it shut with a loud bang.

And there goes the rest of my appetite.

Thirteen

Cora

I TREAT TODAY as if I'm getting ready for one of my movie premieres. I start off at the hotel spa with a massage, manicure, and pedicure. Afterwards, I head back to my room where I order room service for lunch, usually something that won't cause me to bloat. I take a warm bath right before I get my hair and makeup done. Once that's complete, it's time to get dressed. I walk to the closet and pull out the silver metallic beaded gown. Even calling it a 'gown' is a huge stretch since it's purely see-through with very little fabric. I slide my robe off, a nude thong the only clothing I have on underneath, and step into the dress. I pull the material up to my fake breasts and take the remaining fabric over my head and place around my neck. I walk to the mirror and smile in satisfaction.

The look of this dress is exactly what I was hoping for. The fashion world calls this type of dress a nude illusion design. The slinky design has detailed beading with a plunging neckline to my belly button, showcasing the insides of my breasts. A thigh-high slit in the front shows off my legs, and the beaded details ends around my hips. The rest of the dress is pure sheerness down to my calves, with my ass in my thong on full display.

Is it a bit much for an at-home birthday party?

Absolutely.

But I always go over the top, wanting everyone to be talking about me.

And I will be the talk of this party.

I slip on my silver metallic pointy heels, put on my emerald, green earrings and bracelet and take one more look in the mirror.

Goddamn, I look good.

I give myself a wink and grab my purse for my last ritual of the evening before heading out. I take my square compact out of my bag and my rolled-up hundred dollar bill. I open up the secret compartment in my purse and pull out the small vile of magic white powder. I pour a little on the compact, make two lines with it, put the makeshift straw at the end of the line, and snort it up my nose to oblivion. I stand up, lean my head back, and take one last sniff. I wipe away any remnants, wash my hands, and go downstairs.

Now I'm ready to conquer the world.

The car Danny rented is waiting for me when I exit the lobby of the hotel. The person he hired is a tall, middle-aged man in decent shape, wearing a black suit with a white button-down shirt and no hat. Satisfied with his look, I nod at him as he opens the door for me to get in.

The highways are smooth for a Saturday with very little traffic. Twenty-five minutes later, we arrive at their gated community where I hand over my identification for the guard to check against the guest list he was provided. The gate opens and we drive to their street, where more security guards are outside of their personal gate checking guests in. I have to admit, it's impressive the amount of security Jenna has for this evening. Sean definitely deserves, at minimum, a kiss for letting me be his plus one.

My driver pulls up to the front of the house. I don't talk to him, so I have no idea where he plans on parking the vehicle in order to get photos of the party. Frankly, I don't care. All that matters is that he takes the photos I need him to take. He opens the door for me and slips me his card with his cell phone number on it while taking my hand to help me out of the car. I watch him drive away and when he's out of sight, I look around to see if anyone was watching us. When I see the coast is clear, I square my shoulders back, hold my head up high, and walk into their house.

Right away I feel people's eyes on me, starting with the catering staff and some of the guests. I plaster a smile on my face and walk toward the kitchen. I see Philip talking to Cal's parents and sisters, which stops me in my tracks.

What in the hell are Cal's family doing here all the way from England?

I wasn't expecting to see them, but I guess it's not that surprising since it's his birthday and he rarely ever gets to celebrate with them. I have met his mum before and this is not the type of dress that's going to make her think you are worthy of her son. In fact, it's quite the opposite. I turn around to detour somewhere else when I hear Philip calling my name. I take a deep breath before I turn back and head in their direction. Their reaction is exactly what I knew this dress would produce—mouths drop open, rendering them speechless. They all stare at me as I make my way to them.

"Cora, whoa … um, you remember Cal's family, right?" He nervously laughs and looks between us, waiting for someone to react.

"Such a pleasure to see you all again." I extend my hand toward his father, but all I get in return is a disdained look.

"Miss Gregory, I do hope you don't catch a chill this evening with your lack of attire," his mother tells me. She looks me square in the eyes before turning to her husband. "Let's go visit with the children. Nice to see you, Philip." They all leave without saying another word to me and head out of the kitchen.

"Have you lost your fucking mind, Cora?" Philip hisses as he grabs my elbow and leads me outside. "What are you hoping to accomplish wearing *that* to Cal's party?"

I remove my elbow from his grasp and innocently shrug my

shoulders. "No one told me what the dress code was, Philip. How was I supposed to know what to properly wear?"

He scoffs, not believing one word of my bullshit.

I ignore him and look around at the outside scenery, taking in the whimsical decor with beautiful flowers, lanterns, and lights hanging off trees and shrubs. Flooring has been placed on top of the pool to be used as a dance floor. There are ten round tables with large flower arrangements in the center of them surrounding both sides of the dance floor and a stage in back that has pipe and drape with a single microphone. A banner saying, "Happy Birthday, Cal" hangs off branches with flowers that decorate the top of the pipe and drape. A DJ is set up at the side of the stage, spinning dinner appropriate music. Buffet tables of food are off to the sides, creating a boxed in like set up around the whole area. Four open bars are stationed at each corner with lines of people chatting and laughing. There are mobile fire pits further onto the property with couches and chairs for guests to sit on to chat. I see familiar faces of other people in the entertainment industry— actors, actresses, stunt doubles, directors, producers, and stylists. All people who Cal has worked closely with presently or in the past. Sean must have helped Jenna with the guest list. I nod at some of them, but most of them ignore me, jealousy and hatred radiating from their eyes.

"I think it might be best that you leave, Cora." Philip stands in front of me, forcing me to look at him. "Your intentions for being here are not good."

I wave my hand at him, dismissing his ridiculous words. "Nonsense, Philip. I'm here to celebrate one of my best friends. Now if you will excuse me, I must go and pay my respects to the hostess."

Respect is the last thing I will be giving Jenna. All I really want to do is go inside the house to snoop around. I attempt to make my way through the increasing crowd when Jenna comes out from inside of the house and stands in the doorway.

"They're pulling into the neighborhood, everyone! The music

is going to be turned off, so I need you to lower your voices to a whisper so Cal doesn't hear you." She's wearing a simple black sheath dress that is wrapped around her waist. Her hair and makeup are professionally done, more sophisticated looking than her ugly dress. Some might think she looks beautiful, but to me, she will always look like a rat. She's smiling at the crowd when her eyes reach mine and she freezes. Her gaze proceeds to move up and down my body, checking out my attire. I make sure to give her a spiteful smile when her eyes reach back to mine. Instead of looking shocked, she smiles even brighter at me and moves forward.

"Cora, how wonderful to see you again!" She says loudly as she wraps her arms around me in a tight hug. I can smell the scent of her floral perfume when she leans in and whispers in my ear softly, "How embarrassing it must be for you to have your stylist make you look so desperate in that dress." My smile falters as her words echo throughout me. The bitch is smarter than I take her for, since it's evident she's doing this on purpose. Everyone is watching us, preventing me from doing what I really want to do to her.

Choke her until every last breath leaves her body.

She pulls back, places her hands around my biceps, and squeezes her nails into my flesh until I have to bite my lips from crying out in pain. That might even leave scars. "You look adorable! Thanks for coming tonight." She finally releases me, motions everyone to be silent and walks to the door, which she closes after entering back into the house. We watch as she pulls the blinds down so Cal can't see out. People start crowding around me, sandwiching me into place while we wait in anticipation for our cue to yell "surprise" when Cal appears.

Our wait is less than ten minutes when the door opens and the magnificent specimen that is Cal Harrington walks through it. He takes a step back from the shock of the surprise, but his eyes light up with happiness. He is wearing a black polo shirt that is pulled tightly against his muscled chest and arms, gray chino pants and black shoes. I can't take my eyes off him; my love, my obsession. My view of him becomes obstructed when people's hands go up in the air to wave and clap. When they finally lower their arms, he is holding his daughter with one arm and his other arm is wrapped around Jenna's waist as she holds their son.

A picture-perfect looking family.

One that I can't wait to destroy.

He puts Avery down and starts to greet his guests as they crowd around him. It is going to be awhile before I can get him alone, so I bide my time and scan the crowd for Sean. I see him in the corner in a heated discussion with Isla. I slowly make my way toward them, trying to read his lips in the process. Looks like he is pleading with her to believe him, that he's not in love with me anymore.

We'll see about that.

"Sean, darling, there you are!" I yell while quickening my pace. I practically throw myself at him, wrapping my arms around his neck. He has to hold onto me in order for us not to topple backwards. He tries to pull away from me as soon as he regains his balance, but I grab his face and kiss him with all the passion I have from just seeing Cal, pretending it's his lips and not Sean's. His lips open in surprise and I sweep my tongue through them. He tries to break free of my grasp, but I move my hands to his shoulders and squeeze tightly, making sure Isla sees every thrust of my tongue into his mouth. He tastes good. Real good and I can actually feel desire pooling in my core.

Not being able to withstand the force of his strength any longer, he pushes me away from him. "Enough, Cora! What in the hell do you think you're doing?" He roars, his breath coming out in gasps as he tries to regain his composure.

"I'm sorry, darling, but I just missed you from last night." I give him a coy look as I slip my arm around him and grope his ass. He slaps my hand away in anger and I can't contain the smile on my face.

"You two disgust me!" Isla hisses before she tries to walk

away. Sean reaches out to grab her wrist, but she manages to break free before he can get a firm grasp on it. "Don't touch me!" She cries out and walks toward Jenna. She whispers something in Jenna's ear, who nods, and goes with Isla and the children into the house.

"Awe, did I interrupt a lover's spat with the nanny?" I tease before crying out in pain from the grip of Sean's hand wrapped around my forearm while he drags me to a more remote area closer to the stage.

"What the fuck kind of game are you playing, Cora?" He pushes me away from him and I start to rub at the pain from his death grip. His eyes are blazing with rage, his hands fisted at his side. I don't think I've ever seen Sean this angry before.

For once, fear creeps into me.

"I'm sorry, Sean, but I did miss you. I've been thinking more and more about the idea of us together," I plead as I try to reach for him, but he holds up his hands to stop me. "I think we should finally take that next step, Sean. We had so much fun making this last movie together and it made me realize that you have always been there for me, Sean. You have always been taking care of me, protecting me. It makes me realize that we've wasted so much time being apart. I'm ready to be yours."

"No," he growls in a low voice as he shakes his head. "I don't believe you. Look at you," he motions his hand up and down, gesturing towards my dress. "You look like a high-class whore!"

I gasp and put my hand over my heart, pretending he has wounded me, when inside I'm seething at his choice words. *How dare he call me a whore!* "Oh Sean, but I wore this for you! How can you say such hurtful things to me? I thought you would like this on me."

He reaches up and grasps my jaw, making my teeth clench while his fingers dig into it. His eyes are hard and cruel as he inches closer to my face. "Such lies that come out of that beautiful, deceitful mouth of yours. I'm seeing clearly for once the venom that you spit out and I'm done with it." He pushes my face away from his and releases me, causing me to stumble backwards. He turns his back on me and rakes both hands through his hair, before turning back around to face me. "I want you gone, now!"

He stalks toward me and takes my elbow to lead me away, but I manage to yank my arm free from his grasp. "No, Sean, you don't mean that! I know you don't really mean it! Besides, I can't leave without saying hello to Cal."

"Cal doesn't even want you here!" He tells me while grabbing my wrist. He's about to continue his verbal assault when we hear a loud tapping noise and turn to see Robert standing at the microphone.

"Ladies and Gentlemen, if you can quickly grab something to eat and drink and take it to your seats, we would like to start our celebration." I look at Sean and he places his hand on my lower back, pushing me to the closest table for us to sit down at.

"As soon as the speeches are done, you are leaving," he commands, his eyes scanning the crowd until it stops. I look to see him watching Robert escort Isla, the children, Jenna's parents and Cal's family to the two tables in front of us, closest to the stage. Jenna's best friend, Layla, and her fiancé, Chase, also sit down with them. Once they're all seated, Robert gets back up on stage to talk with the DJ before returning to the microphone.

"Do you know what's happening?" I ask Sean, looking around for Cal, but not finding him. There are still people walking outside from the house, so he's probably still talking with guests.

"I was not privy to the schedule of events for the birthday party. Rightfully so since I made a horrible mistake inviting you here."

I ignore Sean and focus my attention on Robert as he clinks a knife to his glass of champagne to get everyone's attention. Obviously the flutes of champagne on the tables are for a toast to Cal, but I have zero hesitations downing my glass now and signaling the waiter for another one.

"Hello and welcome everyone! We're so happy and honored

that you could join us tonight in celebrating the birth of Cal Harrington. A big thank you to his parents for creating such a real-life Adonis." The crowd laughs and joins Robert in applauding the Harringtons, who stand up out of their seats to wave, their cheeks flushed from embarrassment.

"Jenna and I have worked really hard on making sure this party was a surprise and we couldn't have done it without you all, so give yourself a round of applause for being able to keep a secret!" I roll my eyes at everyone applauding themselves and continue looking around for Cal. Usually wherever Jenna is, Cal is, but I'm not seeing either of them. Suspicion starts to kick in, making me wonder why Robert is out here giving a speech without the guest of honor.

"When Cal told us what he wanted for his birthday, I laughed in his face and told him he needs to forget about it. So instead, Jenna and I schemed up the plan for a party. Good thing it's also what we do for a living," Robert jokes, the crowd laughing with him at his reference to his and Jenna's event planning business. "But wishes do come true and Jenna decided to give Cal what he has been asking for. Ladies and Gentlemen, the surprise is actually on *you*! I'm ecstatic to really welcome you to the surprise wedding between Cal and Jenna!"

"*No!*" I gasp in horror, feeling as if the air is being sucked out of my lungs. Catering staff descend upon the stage, removing the banner and take down the pipe and drape, revealing two large walls filled from top to bottom with white, cream and pale pink peonies. The crowd murmurs their excitement and starts to cheer as Cal comes into view from the far-right side of the backyard. He has changed into a slim-fit navy-blue suit with a crisp white button-down shirt underneath and black dress shoes on his feet. He comes onto the stage, hugs Robert, and waves to the crowd. My eyes are immediately drawn to the pale pink peony boutonniere that is fixed to his jacket lapel.

"Did you know about this?" I turn sharply to look at Sean, but notice the equally shocked expression on his face. Jenna and

Cal were supposed to get married last fall, but she postponed it due to the arrival of Brooks. No rescheduled date was ever announced.

"I was completely left out of the dark on this one. Holy shit, I can't believe they've pulled this off. They are finally getting married!" He turns to look at me with a smile of excitement, but that quickly dissipates when he notices my look of disgust.

This has got to be some sort of cruel joke.

It's supposed to be a birthday party, not a wedding!

I watch Cal as he blows kisses to his children and family before standing on his marker on stage. He looks at the door to the house, staring at it with intense anticipation.

I must stop this.

I lurch up out of my seat, ready to go talk some sense into Cal, when large hands roughly grab my hips and painfully push me back down into my seat. Sean wraps his left arm around me, his hand grabbing my forearm and forcing it onto the top of the table. He hauls my right side into his hard chest, squeezing me into him.

"Let me go, Sean!" I try pushing at him, but it's as if I'm pushing against a brick wall. Panic starts to seize me at the thought of having to watch this horrible nightmare. "I just want to go congratulate Cal," I lie, my voice unsteady from the nervous breakdown that I'm about to have. The people at our table turn to give us weird looks, but their focus is drawn back to the stage when a small ensemble of four men start to play *A Thousand Years* with their string instruments. All eyes focus on the door to the house, but mine are trained on Cal. His eyes reveal the moment Jenna has come into his view as they start to sparkle with unabashed desire, his full lips breaking into a breathtaking smile filled with love and happiness that makes me inhale sharply. It's a look I've never seen on his face for as long as I have known him.

Like a slow-moving train wreck that you can't help but watch, Jenna enters my view, slowly walking toward the stage to marry the man that is supposed to be mine. She's wearing an off the shoulder, white bohemian mermaid-style fitted lace wedding dress with a slit up the front and a sweetheart neckline that shows the top of her breasts. Her caramel-colored hair is styled down in long waves, her makeup heavy on the eyes with pale pink lipstick shimmering on her lips. She's carrying a large pale pink peony bouquet that she hands to Avery before climbing the stairs to join Cal. She stands in front of him and he grabs her hands, squeezing them in encouragement. *You are the most beautiful woman I have ever seen*, he mouths right before Robert starts officiating.

This really is a wedding and not a birthday party.

This can't be happening to me!

He's getting married and it isn't to me!

I attempt one more time to get out of my seat, but Sean only tightens his grip on me. "You will sit here and watch the person you call your best friend marry the woman of his dreams," he whispers with malice into my ear. "You will not make a fucking sound or I will drag you inside the house and strangle you myself." I look around in shock as reality starts to grip my heart and squeezes the life out of it once Robert starts talking about why God intended for the union between Cal and Jenna.

My heart goes numb when Jenna says her vows, telling Cal he is her forever soulmate.

My heart starts cracking when Cal says his vows, telling Jenna that she, and no one else, was made for him.

And my heart finally shatters into a million pieces when they are officially pronounced man and wife. Cal lifts Jenna off the ground in a bear hug and crushes his mouth to hers, their tongues lost inside of each other as their mouths fuse together to become one.

The noise of the crowd's cheers is deafening and Sean has to pull me up to stand when everyone rises to watch Cal and Jenna make their way off the stage to go back into the house to have a private moment with their immediate family.

"Now you know exactly what it feels like to officially not be wanted by the one person you want the most." Sean's words break me out of my trance and as soon as I feel his grip loosen, I bolt for the house, needing to remove myself as far away as possible before I do something to get myself arrested. The crowd blocks my way toward the main entrance back into the house, so I run to the sliding glass doors that leads into the kitchen.

"We need to leave now!" I bark into my cell phone when my driver picks up. I hang up on him before opening the doors and I make my way through the kitchen. I stop short when I see a tray filled with champagne in flute glasses waiting by the door to be taken out. Without caring who sees, I deliberately push the tray off the table, the sounds of glass breaking bringing some satisfaction to my black, cold heart.

I ignore the shouts behind me as I run through the foyer and exit the main door. I continue toward the street where all the cars are parked and I don't stop running until I see the SUV I came in. The driver already has the car turned on and opens the door for me as soon as I reach it.

"Hurry, we need to get out of here." I grab the handle of the door while he races around the car to get in. The tires burn rubber as the car races to get out of the neighborhood. I turn around to look out the window as we move farther away from the house. Tears that I never knew I could even produce start leaking out of my eyes and down my cheeks when the house disappears out of my view. I face forward and cry harder as the replay of events from the past thirty minutes flash through my brain.

"I got photos of the whole wedding! Did you know about it?" My driver asks, excitement lighting up his eyes when he looks at me through the rearview mirror. This type of story is going to make him a lot of money.

"Do I look like I fucking knew about it?" I hiss, black mascara streaming down my face from my tears while my heart grieves for the loss of the love of my life.

"Chill the fuck out. Just because they're married doesn't

mean it's the end all be all." The driver looks at me with disgust and focuses his attention back on the road.

At first, I'm insulted by his tone. *How dare he talk to me that way!* But then his words start resonating within me and as the city's skyline comes into view, I calm down and clear my mind.

Marriages can end as quickly as they started.

I still have a press tour to do with Cal.

One that will have moments of Jenna not being around.

A smile of hope plays on my lips as I realize that the driver is right and I start to put a plan into motion.

This press tour is my last shot at making Cal mine and I don't plan on blowing it.

Fourteen

Isla

"MY MOMMY LOOKED like a princess tonight, didn't she, Izzy?" Avery murmurs in her sleepy voice while I carry her up the stairs to her room.

"She sure did, Avery Boo," I grunt out as I make it to the last step of the stairs, which is no small task carrying around an extra fifty pounds and having little arms wrapped around your neck, suffocating you.

It's way past Avery's bed time, but well worth it since we're celebrating her parents' wedding. Not many kids get to be part of that experience and Avery took full advantage of it. While I put her brother to bed after family photos were done, Avery got to stay up to enjoy the party. When I arrived back downstairs, she was the center of attention on the dance floor with her family and their friends. She was having the time of her life, but when Jenna said it was time for her to finally go to bed, she was delirious with exhaustion and didn't even attempt to argue with her mother.

"Will I be as pretty as my mommy when I'm an adult, Izzy?" I set her down in front of me and help get her out of her dress and into her pajamas.

"Absolutely, but what does your mommy tell you about being pretty, Avery?" I walk her to her bathroom and get her toothbrush ready for her. She can do all of this herself, but she's moving at a snail's pace and I'm afraid she might just plop on the floor and call it a night if we don't speed up the bedtime process.

"If you're pretty on the inside by being kind and respectful, then you're pretty on the outside too," she mutters before I stick the toothbrush into her mouth and brush her teeth for her. Less than five minutes after tucking her in, she's dreaming about rainbows and unicorns. I shut her door softly and am about to go to my own room, when my phone buzzes with a text message from Robert.

Robert: Come down to the right side fire pit and hang out with us.

The time on my cell phone says it's ten o'clock and with the noise level from outside as loud as it is, the party does not seem to be slowing down anytime soon. Attempting to go to bed would be pointless, so I make my way back downstairs to join the party.

The DJ is playing the latest electronic dance music and the dance floor is packed. I get a glimpse of Jenna dancing with Cal's sisters as I walk past them toward the fire pit. Cal, Robert, Kellan, Sean, Chase, and Layla are sitting around the fire, drinking and telling stories when I arrive.

"Isla, were the kids okay?" Cal questions with concern laced in his voice. He is holding a glass of bourbon, his new piece of hardware on his left hand shining in the light of the fire.

"They were so exhausted from the excitement of tonight. Can't blame them, really. *I'm* tired from the excitement of tonight!" I laugh, shaking my head in astonishment still from the surprise. "Why did you guys not tell any of us?"

"We had to tell Robert, because we wanted him to get ordained in order to marry us. Plus, Jenna needed help planning it." He looks down at his ring, a faint smile touching his lips. "We've actually been legally married for a month now."

"*What?*" Robert and Layla shriek in shock, indicating that this is news to both of them. Robert and Layla are Jenna's closest friends. I can't even begin to imagine how hard it was for Jenna not to tell them.

"Seriously, Cal? You couldn't even tell *me* about this?" Sean actually looks hurt by the news and a part of me feels bad for him. The smallest of parts since I'm still pissed at him for going to dinner with Cora the other night. Not that it's any of my business, but it makes it hard for me to take him seriously about being over her.

"It's nothing personal, Sean." Cal tells him before looking over at Robert. "Remember that day when I came to the offices downtown to meet Jenna for lunch?" Robert nods his head at the memory. "Do you remember how happy I was when we returned?"

"Yes, but I just figured you guys had a quickie at Jenna's old condo."

"Well, of course we did," Cal says nonchalantly, "but the night before, I asked her why she wouldn't marry me. She just shrugged her shoulders and responded back with who said that she wouldn't? I thought she was bluffing, so I decided to test her and when I picked her up for lunch that next day, I took her straight to the courthouse to see how she would react. To my surprise, she grabbed my hand and marched us into the City Clerk's office and an hour later, we were legally married."

"Wow," I whisper in awe at how romantic the story is and how much in love Cal really is with Jenna. That's exactly the kind of love I want to find. But that kind of love is one in a million and usually doesn't come easy. It didn't for Cal and Jenna.

"Why didn't you guys at least tell us that? I feel deceived." Robert pouts, looking like a child who was just denied candy.

"Because we wanted to have something to ourselves for once. With our life being so public, I'm shocked that the news didn't even get out with marriage licenses being public record."

"Why keep the wedding a surprise though? I'm still upset that I didn't get to be maid of honor," Layla says, while snuggling closer to Chase, whose arm is around her shoulders.

"We were worried that if it was public knowledge, some people might try to stop it." Cal looks uneasily at Sean, who looks down at his beer bottle and fiddles with the label.

"If you're referring to Cora, I heard she made quite a mess in the kitchen." Kellan tells the story about the event staff seeing her push off the tray of champagne glasses from the table. I look over at Sean, my eyes questioning him in silence. He meets my gaze and shrugs before taking a sip from his beer. "So keeping the wedding a secret was probably a smart decision."

"Are you guys going on a honeymoon?" I ask in curiosity. Cal and Jenna mentioned they have travel arrangements before the next press tour, but kept it vague as to where the location was and if the kids and I were going with them.

"Yes, we are. We'll be leaving for Bora Bora on Tuesday, but before then, we will be escorting you, the kids, and my family to Disneyland." Cal smiles at me when my mouth drops open in shock for the second time tonight.

"Are we really going to Disneyland?" I whisper since that is the one place I've never been to and have always wanted to go. The inner child in me is jumping for joy, but what I'm really excited about is how Avery will react.

"We will leave Monday and go straight there, because Jenna and I don't want to miss seeing Avery's reaction. We will spend the whole day there and then Jenna and I will fly out Tuesday for five glorious days in an expensive hut in the middle of the ocean where we will work hard at populating this world with more Harringtons." We all laugh at Cal, knowing that Jenna isn't receptive to the idea of having another baby just yet … or ever again.

"Good luck persuading Jenna to stop taking her birth control," Robert laughs sarcastically. "That woman used to make sure she popped that pill exactly at the same time every day."

"That won't be an obstacle." Cal shrugs his shoulders, determination set in his eyes. "I plan on wearing her out so much that she won't hear her cell phone alarm going off with her reminder." I laugh at the arrogance in his voice, but I have no doubt that the man fully plans on executing his plan of wearing

Jenna out sexually, especially since there won't be any children around to distract her.

"While that might seem like a good plan, what if she has the new kind of birth control that gets inserted inside of you?" Layla questions Cal with a raised eyebrow.

"I have checked that area very thoroughly and I can assure you she has nothing inserted inside of her." He smirks while Robert makes gagging noises at the mental image that is going through his brain.

"Too much information, but there are other areas you can insert birth control in, like your arm."

"What freaky ass science experiment is that?" Kellan exclaims, his face distorted in disgust. "Why would women do that to themselves?"

"Because some women aren't good at remembering to take pills every day, let alone setting an alarm to remind them," Layla responds and I'm wondering if she's one of those women with the way she sheepishly looks at Chase. I, on the other hand, am like Jenna and make it a priority to take mine every single day, despite not currently being in a sexual relationship.

"Jenna's too granola for that shit, right Cal?" All eyes go to Cal, who actually has a look of doubt on his face.

"Would you be able to feel it in her arm if she does have one?" Cal pulls out his phone to start researching it.

"I think I heard that you can," I respond and we all laugh at the look on Cal's face as he gets up and walks over to where his wife is located on the dance floor. He starts dancing behind her, but his awkward groping of her biceps makes her turn around with a quizzical look at him. The scene unfolding makes us laugh harder as they both stop dancing and he inspects her biceps more closely. When Cal finishes his inspection, he smiles brightly at her, grabs her, and kisses her while his hands make their way toward her backside to bring her closer against him. The DJ decides to play a slow song and we watch as Cal and Jenna gaze into each other's eyes as the outside world fades for them.

"Dance with me." The words are commanded huskily into my ear from behind, causing me to jump. I didn't notice or hear Sean get up and walk behind my chair. As I stare into his moss-colored eyes, I feel my will power slipping. I don't know if it's because of my body's reaction to him or because we're at a wedding, but I want to dance. I want to be held in someone's arms. So I nod and place my hand in his while he helps me up and leads me to the dance floor.

I place my left hand on his shoulder while he takes my right hand into his warm, strong one. I feel his other fingers digging into the small of my back as he brings me right into his chest. My nipples stand to attention when they come in contact with him. He smells like home, making me struggle in refraining from closing my eyes and inhaling his scent. I swallow the lump of lust in my throat when he brings our hands to rest over his heart.

"Are you okay tonight?" I quietly ask, needing to start some sort of conversation with him to distract my hand from rubbing up and down his chest.

"Yeah, I'm fine. I understand why Cal didn't tell me anything."

"I didn't mean about Cal, I meant about Cora." I meet his gaze, wanting to watch his eyes while I say her name. Hurt and betrayal briefly flash through them before he puts his acting mask back on. He gives me a sad smile and shakes his head.

"I don't know who Cora is anymore. Maybe I never truly did know her. Maybe I have just been blinded by my feelings for her. But I'm not blind anymore, Isla." He releases his hand from mine to caress my cheek. I close my eyes, relishing in the pleasure of his touch, needing it to continue. I open my eyes to see his fixated on my lips. He takes his thumb and gently rubs it against my lower lip, causing my lips to part. My breath exhales as I debate whether or not to suck on it.

"Ladies and Gentlemen, this will be the last song of the evening. So let's make it memorable!" The DJ announces as he plays *Crazy In Love* by Beyonce.

"Spend the night with me, Isla," Sean demands while we look

into each other's eyes, slowly swaying together to the beat of our hearts and not the music. I believe him when he says he's trying to get over Cora, but in no way do I want to be just a rebound for him. He sees my hesitation as I look away from him to contemplate the idea. He grabs my chin between his fingers, forcing me to look up at him. "I just want to hold you, Isla. That's all I want for tonight at least."

The idea that Sean wants more nights with me makes my heart soar, despite the warning bells going off inside of me, the ones screaming that I need to stay away from him.

But I'm tired of staying away from Sean Lindsey.

I nod and he presses his forehead against mine, closing his eyes. "Thank you," he whispers before kissing my forehead. He takes my hand and walks us to the house. We continue in silence to his room, which is conveniently located far away from the rest of the bedrooms in the house. He opens the door, flicks the lights on, and closes the door after I follow him in. My feet refuse to move as I stand frozen in place, suddenly feeling awkward being alone in his room with him. He walks around me to the dresser and pulls out a white t-shirt. He comes over and stands right in front of me, his eyes raking over the dark green dress I'm wearing.

"Here's a shirt for you to sleep in. It should be long enough on you." I grab the shirt from him and head to his bathroom. I use his toothbrush, but don't dare take off my makeup, hoping that I won't look like a raccoon in the morning. I take off my dress and bra, but leave my thong on. I pull the shirt over my head and see that it barely reaches the top of my thighs. I want to try to stretch the shirt past my knees, but it isn't my shirt to do that to. I debate whether or not to put my bra back on with the way my nipples are playing peekaboo through the material.

Screw that, I want Sean to want me.

I open the door to see Sean sitting on his bed, the only thing he's wearing is his boxer briefs. He rises and moves slowly toward me, my breath hitching as my eyes take in his six pack, moving down to his muscled lines that disappears into his underwear. The room feels stiflingly hot from the lust that has taken over my body. My gaze makes its way back up to his face to see his eyes fixated on my breasts. I know he can see how hard my nipples are with the way they ache to be touched.

"You look damn fucking sexy in my shirt," he mutters and stops only inches away from me. "Get into bed, I'll be right there." He walks past me into the bathroom and closes the door.

I pull back the blanket and get in, the coldness of the sheets against my legs causing me to shiver. I bring the comforter all the way to my chin, feeling self-conscious about not having more clothes on. I rub my thighs together, the friction of my thong against my core reminding me just how thin the piece of material is and that it's the only barrier covering the one place that is dying to be touched by him.

I hear the door to the bathroom open and follow Sean's movement when he walks to the light switch to turn off the lights. The room is engulfed in darkness, the only light being from the moon shining in between the cracks of the curtains. I make out Sean's silhouette while he walks around to his side of the bed. I keep staring at the chandelier hanging from the ceiling, even when I feel the bed dip from his weight.

"Turn on your side, facing the other way." I do as he commands and he wraps his arms around my waist and pulls me against him. My back collides with his chest and I feel his hot breath against my neck while he inhales my scent. Wetness pools at my core and I push my ass against his growing erection. He inhales sharply and gently nips at my shoulder with his teeth. "Stop moving or I won't be able to keep my promise of holding you while we sleep."

I smile into the darkness, feeling powerful in knowing that I can make his body react to me. I sigh in contentment and squeeze his forearms as they wrap tighter around me.

"Sweet dreams, my little Izzy," he murmurs, his voice gruff with sleepiness.

For once in a very long time, I don't hate hearing the sound of my nickname from him anymore.

Fifteen

Sean

THE ACHING THROB coming from my dick causes me to moan out in discomfort as I open my eyes to get a bearing of my surroundings. I'm lying on my stomach. my arm draped over Isla's waist while she's on her back, fast asleep. Her face is turned away from me, the scent of her floral shampoo annihilating my senses. I lift my upper body up and rest on my forearms to reach for my phone to see that it is six in the morning. Isla will need to go soon if she doesn't want anyone to see her walking from my room. I lie back down and watch her as she sleeps. She looks so beautiful, so peaceful. It's as if an angel has graced me with her presence.

My eyes leave her face and notice that her shirt has bunched up around her stomach. I see glimpses of a tight tummy, her nude thong covering up what I'm really interested in seeing. I can't help the wicked smile that crosses my face as I think of the perfect way to wake Izzy up.

I lift up the covers and gently push them down toward the end of the bed. My hands softly touch her stomach, my finger circling gently around her belly button. I lightly trail my fingers up, bringing her shirt along with them, exposing the bottom of her breasts. I lift the shirt higher and my cock hardens at the sight of her beautiful, pink nipples. I rub the pad of my thumb against the bud and watch in desire while it hardens under my touch.

Unable to help myself, I take that nipple into my mouth, groaning softly at how delicious it tastes. Isla moves her legs, her head thrashing back and forth while I slowly attack her nipple. I move my body closer, placing my right hand on the other side of her waist. I release her nipple, kiss up and down her sternum, and give my attention to her other breast. This time she whimpers and runs her hands through my hair. "Sean?" The question in her voice makes me look up to see her eyes filled with passion. That's all the encouragement I need to continue making my way down her body. "What are you doing?"

"Helping you wake up so you can start your day off right," I murmur in between kisses against her abdomen. I get to the valley in between her legs and stick my nose against her clit, using the material of her underwear to cause friction. She moans loudly and opens her legs up to accommodate me better. I kiss the inside of each thigh, noting one of her sensitive spots when she jerks against my touch. My attention zeros in on her core and I push aside her thong with one hand and use the other hand to spread her wide. I nestle my chin into her opening as my tongue slowly moves up and down her most sensitive area. I moan into her, never before tasting someone as good as she tastes.

"Sean," she seductively pants, her fingers gripping my hair tight while she pushes my head harder into her. My tongue continues its assault as I stick two fingers inside her, my cock twitching when I feel her walls tighten around them. I slowly move my fingers in a circle, then start gliding them in and out, exactly how I imagine I would with my dick. With the way she keeps pulsating around my fingers, it's not going to take her long to come. I pick up the pace with both my tongue and fingers as her hips start to move to the same rhythm. When her moaning becomes more frequent, I remove my fingers and put all of my concentration on her clit. Her thighs tighten around my head and her pelvis moves fast against me. I grab her hips and bury my tongue deeper, lapping her up as fast as I can. This seems to bring her over the edge and I have to cover her mouth with my free hand to drown out her screams of pleasure as she explodes from her orgasm.

I continue licking at her until her body starts twitching and she pushes my head away from her overstimulated bud. I get up to see her chest heaving up and down from being breathless, her arm draped over her eyes, preventing me from seeing them. Her lips are swollen from her biting them, making me grin with egotistical satisfaction. I get off of the bed and walk toward the bathroom. I shut the door and start the shower, needing to provide immediate relief to my erection. As soon as I get in the shower, I grip my cock and work my hands up and down, imaging being inside her. I quietly come fast, knowing that it wasn't going to take long since I can still taste her on my lips. I quickly wash my face, body, and hair and pop right out of the shower. Just the thought of her still lying in bed makes me ready for a repeat performance. I wrap a towel around me and go back out to join her.

Disappointment douses my excitement when I see that the bed is empty, her folded up dress gone, and in its place is my white shirt. I grab my phone to text her when I notice I have two missed texts already. One from Cora and the other from Cal.

Cora: We need to talk. I would like to apologize for last night. Can you please meet me before I board my flight home?

I re-read her text message again, making sure my eyes are not deceiving me since Cora never apologizes for anything. I decide to postpone responding back to her and click over to read Cal's text message.

Cal: I need to talk to you. Can you come meet me in my office?

Shit, I hope he didn't see Izzy come out of my room. I respond back, saying I'll be down in five minutes and quickly get dressed, but before I leave, I send Isla a text.

Me: Good morning, beautiful! I wish you didn't leave me while I was in the shower, but I understand you wanted to get to your room before anyone saw you. I hope to spend more time with you tonight.

I decide a cup of coffee is needed before I see Cal, so I go to the kitchen first, hoping I get to see Izzy. Unfortunately, the kitchen was empty and I had to brew my own cup of coffee because no one had started the pot yet. I pour myself and Cal a cup and walk to his office.

He's staring at his computer screen when I enter, captivated by whatever he's watching. He's shirtless, wearing only his pajama pants, making it evident that he came straight here once he woke up.

"You might scare your employees showing off your ugly body like that," I tease and set his cup of coffee down in front of him. Cal's body is anything but ugly, being the envy of most men. There are hundreds of gifs and memes of him shirtless on the internet, the scenes pulled from some of his past movies. I have no doubt most of those were created by women.

"Since it's Sunday, that would only apply to Isla and it's her day off."

"She's gone already?" Shock registers on my face and he tilts his head to the side, looking at me inquisitively.

"You tell me, Sean. Is she gone already? Don't think we all didn't notice your disappearance last night."

"I honestly don't know where Isla is right now," I answer truthfully. I choose my words carefully to not give away that I used to know where she was earlier.

He stares at me in silence, doubt showing through his eyes. "Let's discuss the real reason why I asked you to come into my office. I wanted to show you the video surveillance from last night."

I move around the desk to stand behind him. The video camera from the far corner of the living room gives you visible access to the whole room, including the entrance into the kitchen. Cal hits play and after a few seconds, Cora appears, her face visibly distraught. We watch her make her way into the living room, look down at the tray of champagne glasses, and purposely push the tray off the table.

"So the story is true." I narrow my eyes at the monitor, making sure I'm seeing exactly what I think I'm seeing. I didn't want to believe that Cora would do this, but the evidence is right in front of me.

"Appears so, but sadly, that isn't what bothers me the most. Check this out." He clicks out of that screen and brings up another video from outside of the house. The recording comes from the camera that is posted on top of their front entrance gate. We see a black SUV come up to the gate and watch a middle-aged man come out and open up the back passenger door closest to Cal's driveway. Cora quickly enters the scene, gets into the car, and her car door is slammed shut. The driver races around the other side of the car and drives away. Cal rewinds a few frames back and pauses the video on the driver. He zooms in so we can get a better look at his face.

"Take a good look at this guy. Have you seen him before?"

I rack my brain, trying to recollect if I have ever encountered him before as a driver, but I'm drawing blanks. "No, I don't think I have."

Cal minimizes that video and pulls forward another one, this video of the side of the house. All I see are hedges coming up to the top of their fence, but Cal pauses the video and zooms in on a specific object. He crops the object out of the freeze frame and then zooms in some more. We can now see the side of the man's head with a super wide lens camera. As Cal zooms in some more, the guy resembles Cora's driver.

"No way!" I stare in disbelief at the screen. "Cora's driver is taking photos of the party?"

"We are the number one trending topic this morning." He pulls up his internet browser where he has multiple tabs opened to various gossip columnists, all showcasing photos from his wedding that was less than twelve hours ago.

I blink a couple of times to regain my vision from staring so intently at the screen and look at Cal. He seems upset, but I have a feeling it's not because his wedding is all over the news. "Do you think Cora knew about this?"

"I got the license plate number of the car from the main entrance security guard and the vehicle is registered to a rental company, not to a transportation company." I suddenly feel sick to my stomach as to what Cal is implying. I refuse to believe that Cora would do that to someone she's supposedly in love with.

"She wouldn't do that, Cal," I say firmly, trying to squash my doubts that are screaming like smoke detector sirens going off. When there's smoke, there's usually fire, and this fire might be in the form of Cora Gregory.

"How do you know that? I never would have thought she would tip over a tray of glasses out of spite at my own wedding, but she did. There's no excuse for her behavior, Sean. I think she's on drugs. Her mood swings are uncontrollable and she's thinner than ever."

There have been rumors for years of people saying that Cora uses cocaine. I questioned her once about it, but she vehemently denied it, saying she wouldn't jeopardize her career that way. Since I've never personally seen her partake in it, especially with the amount of time we spent together on our last movie, I accepted her answer.

And now I feel like a fool for believing her.

Her drug use would explain her erratic behavior. She has always been thin, but I believe that has been ingrained into her since she was a child, courtesy of her mother. Appearances have always been a number one priority for Cora's mother. I sigh heavily and decide to sit down. As I walk around Cal's desk to one of his chairs, I suddenly feel overwhelmingly tired.

"So what do you want to do, Cal? Stage an intervention? She texted me this morning, asking if I would come meet her so she could apologize. Did you get the same text?"

"She asked if she could come over to apologize, but I told her no, that she was no longer welcome in my house." He stares one more time at the computer screen before leaning back in his chair, his gaze staring outside of the window closest to him. He is lost in thought for a brief moment before turning his attention back to me.

"I think after our press tour, I need to file a restraining order against her."

I sit up straighter in my chair, his words sending shock waves down my spine. "What? Cal, no! That's not what friends do, especially with how long all of us have been friends for. That drastic action might put her over the edge, making her feel outcasted by you."

"Sean, I don't trust her around my family. She has been nothing but disrespectful to Jenna from day one. She always shows her disdain for my children whenever she's around them. Any act of kindness is fake. She can't even pretend to be happy for me. If it wasn't for you yesterday sitting with her, who knows what kind of stunt she would've pulled."

If it wasn't for me, she wouldn't have been at the wedding in the first place.

"I had to keep my wedding a goddamn secret from everyone just so she wouldn't ruin it!" He pounds his fist into his desk, his eyes blazing with anger.

"You don't know that she would've done something to ruin it. Maybe she was hurt that she didn't know about it? I know I was a little bothered by not being involved." I shrug, trying to play devil's advocate so that he can maybe put himself in our shoes about being left out from the details of his wedding. "I didn't even get to be your best man."

He leans forward and places his forearms on top of his desk. "Sean, you've been my best man for close to twenty years now. No one else has had the privilege of that title. Cora never even came close to being my best friend. I didn't mean to hurt your feelings, but I have no regrets about not including you in the wedding planning."

I slowly nod my head in understanding, since I know Cal would never do or say anything to intentionally hurt me. Our bond is thick as thieves and although we aren't related by blood, we have always considered ourselves brothers.

"Cal, let me go talk to her today and see what she says. She's going back home until the press tour. Let's see if she lays low and how she acts during the tour. If you feel you still need to file a restraining order by the end of it, then do it."

He analyzes my intentions with his normal intense stare. He looks at his computer screen once more before nodding to me. "Okay, I'll go with your advice. But Sean, I need you to start paying closer attention to her. Pay attention to what she says, what she asks about me, what her next move is. Can you do that for me?"

"Absolutely!" I answer firmly, determined to get to the bottom of Cora and her actions.

"Thank you," he responds and I visibly see his shoulders relax. "Be careful though, Sean. You don't need to fall deeper into her rabbit hole."

"I have no intentions of going back into any of her holes. Not that I literally have ever been into one of her holes," I smirk at him, trying to lighten the mood with a joke. He shakes his head at me, but not before I see the corner of his lips raise up in a half smile. I use this opportunity to change the subject since we have a plan on how to deal with Cora.

"Since you mentioned last night your honeymoon plans for next week, I was thinking that it might be a good idea for me to go to Disneyland with your family while you're gone."

His eyes narrow and he smirks. "Is that so? And why is that?" he asks in amusement and places his hands behind his head. This time I get a knowing smile from him since he knows exactly why I want to go to Disneyland with his family.

"Isla has never really spent alone time with your family like I have, so it might be nice for her to have a familiar face around, helping her with the kids, and being a nice buffer. Also another male presence might make her feel safe since there is so much estrogen in your family."

"My father and two brothers-in-law will be in attendance, not to mention the bodyguards who will be with everyone. If my math serves me correctly, that means there will be more testosterone than estrogen on this trip. Any other reason you might want to be going?"

"How about the fact that I've never met Mickey Mouse in person before and you would be making all of your best friend's childhood dreams come true?" He rolls his eyes and chuckles at my response.

"Let me talk to Jenna and see what she thinks. But, if she says yes, you keep your hands to yourself in front of my kids, you've got that?" He points his finger at me in stern warning.

"Don't worry, I will not grope Mickey Mouse in front of them. Only when they aren't looking." I mock salute him, before turning around to leave his office. I pull out my phone and respond back to Cora, agreeing to meet her for lunch. Hoping there won't be any paparazzi around, but not taking any chances, I decide to tell Isla about what is in store for today.

Me: I forgot that today's your day off. I was hoping to spend the day with you, but I actually need to have a serious conversation with Cora, per Cal's request. I would like to tell you all about it over dinner. Can I pick you up at seven tonight?

I retreat back to my room, wanting to do my own investigating work into Cora before meeting with her. I sit down on my bed with my laptop, stack a couple of pillows behind my back and lean into them. When I do, I catch a whiff of Isla's floral scent, making me smile from the memories of this morning. I decide to not waste my time on looking up Cora on the internet and instead, search for the perfect place to take Isla for dinner tonight because I'm not taking no for an answer from her.

Sixteen

Cora

CAL'S REJECTION TO my request to apologize in person this morning sends me into a downward spiral of rage, making me break anything that I can get my hands on in my apartment. *How dare he ban me from his home! I bet that wasn't even his idea, but hers!* Memories of Jenna in that ugly wedding dress, taking my man from me, fuel my fire in the continuation of destruction. Once my rage finally dissipates, sadness takes its place, and I can't stop my body from slipping to the floor, shaking with uncontrollable sobs. All I have ever wanted in life was to be loved by the people who mean the most to me, but here I am all these years later, alone.

I cry for never receiving the love that I deserved from my father.

I cry for never receiving the love I deserved from my mother.

I cry for losing the man of my dreams.

I cry for having no true friends.

When the tears have all dried up, I look at the sea of broken glass and ceramic that litters my floor, a visual effect of what my heart feels like. I sigh heavily and realize that I'm the one who is going to have to clean up this mess. I stand up to get a broom and dust pan and get to work. The monotony of the sweeping motion of the broom seems to calm me and help lift the fog of misery.

I'm not out of the game *yet*. All I need to do is figure out how to get a photo or video of Cal and me in a compromising position on this upcoming press tour. Evidence will be made public and Jenna will take the kids and leave him, paving the way for us to finally be together. But with his current attitude toward me, that is going to be difficult to orchestrate. Continuing some sort of relationship with Sean is my last hope of keeping ties with Cal. I can only pray that he is more receptive to my message this morning than Cal was. He's slipping through my fingers due to that little slut, Isla. I need to keep myself prevalent in his life, give him more attention, especially physical attention. But how?

My mind's racing at how to handle Sean when my phone alerts me of a text message. I throw the remaining shards of glass in the trash bin, grab my phone, and smile like the Cheshire cat at reading that Sean will see me today. "Yes!" I shout while texting him back a time and location. I walk to my bedroom to figure out what my attire for today should be. Looking through my closet, I decide to keep my outfit casual with a sundress and cardigan. I'm about to start putting makeup on when I realize that it might benefit me to look like I've been crying. I put away my makeup and pull my hair into a tight ponytail. I need to convince Sean that I'm remorseful and that my outburst was because I was feeling like I was losing Cal as a friend since he kept the details of his wedding a secret from us. Sean didn't believe me when I told him I wanted to be with him, so how am I going to convince him that the flipping of the tray with champagne glasses was from anger of feeling left out? My words have lost all credibility, so I need to do something drastic for Sean to believe me. Suddenly, the most brilliant of plans forms in my head. I pick up my cell phone and call my agent because I will need his assistance to pull this off.

"I'm mad at you, Cora, so keep your bullshit short and get to the point of why you are calling," he announces after picking up on the first ring. I can only imagine that the reason he is mad at me is because he knows about my little parting gift last night.

"Philip, I need help," I sob into the phone, hoping that since he's never heard me this way before, that he'll believe my act. "Cal won't talk to me and I don't blame him. What I did last night was unforgivable. I was just so upset that he left us out of his planning of the wedding, that I got angry. But the thought of losing my best friend devastates me even more." I exhale loudly into the phone, creating a dramatic pause before continuing. "I think I need to go to therapy, Philip."

"I'm so relieved to hear you say this, Cora, because I agree, I think you do as well." He sighs into the phone, his voice sounding less harsh than it was a minute ago. "How can I help you with this?"

"I want to go back home to London and enter a week-long treatment facility and then continue with weekly outpatient sessions. Can you help secure that for me, Philip?" I purposely make my voice crack at the end, indicating that I'm about to continue crying. I hold my breath, praying that he's buying all of this since I've never had to act vulnerable before and am unsure if I'm even convincing him. Silence fills the air and then I hear rustling sounds at the end of the receiver.

"Of course, Cora. I can book this for you today."

Hook, line and sinker.

"Oh, Philip, thank you! Thank you for still being my friend!" I dramatically cry out in fake gratitude, pumping my fist in the air for my victory.

"Cora, you're my client. Of course I want what's best for you. Let me make some calls and I will get back to you later when I have more details." I thank him again before hanging up with him. The idea of going home and being in therapy is as appealing as getting a root canal, but this has to be done. Getting Philip involved will convince Sean and Cal that I recognize that I need help.

But in reality, Cal Harrington is the only cure I need for my help.

If they think I'm sincere, the likelihood of them letting me back into their inner circle is high. But this scheme is going to cost me money since I need to pay for the treatment. I also need money because I want Danny Salari with me on this press tour. I need someone to take the incriminating evidence of when I get Cal alone and he's the only one who will do it for me.

This is going to cost me even more money.

Money that I don't have.

The amount of jewelry that I have to sell will not even come close to what it's going to cost me to get Danny to go to Europe with me. I look around, trying to see what else I can sell when it dawns on me that I can sell this apartment. This place was never intended to be permanent and once I make Cal mine, we will want to get a place of our own together.

I call my realtor and tell her I want this place sold as soon as possible. Because it's a buyer's market, I might even make money. Good riddance as I hated being here anyway. It has been a constant reminder of how alone I am.

I go back to my closet and throw all my incognito outfits into the trash. I then go online to book a one-way ticket back to London for tomorrow and text my mother the happy news of my homecoming. Feeling accomplished, I look at the time and see that it's time to go meet Sean. I grab my purse, put on some flats to go with my homely appearance, and make my way downstairs to catch a cab.

I mentally psych myself up for my act with Sean, knowing that I'm going to have to try to make myself cry in order to convince him of my sincerity. My earlier crying session helps because my appearance but I've never had to cry on demand before. It doesn't take us long to arrive at the restaurant. I pay the driver and put my game face on as I get out and head inside.

The hostess leads me to a booth in the very back where Sean is waiting for me. Despite his baseball cap pulled down low to hide his face, you can still tell from his strong jaw line how handsome he really is. Part of me wishes that it was always him I loved, as life would have been a lot easier, but the heart wants what it wants and mine has always wanted Cal.

I slowly sit down across from him and keep my eyes low, giving him a second to observe me before speaking to him. He does exactly what I hope he would do and studies my appearance. I visibly swallow and get ready to perform the most important role of my life.

"Thank you for agreeing to meet me today, Sean. I truly don't think you realize how much I appreciate it." I purposely keep my voice low and slow, swallowing again to make it seem I am holding back tears. "I'm so incredibly sorry for my behavior last night. It was childish and uncalled for."

"Why'd you do it, Cora?" His eyes are cold, his voice emotionless. His body language is screaming that he doesn't even want to be sitting here with me. I need to pick it up a notch, become raw with emotions.

"I did it because I was scared and thought I was losing you both. I was hurt and upset that Cal would keep something so big in his life a secret from us. Then your words to me during the ceremony cut deep. I was angry and wanted to lash out. And unfortunately, I did. If I'm thankful for anything, it's that no one got hurt from the glass." I decide to play on his emotions since I know Sean had to be a little upset from being kept in the dark. "Can you understand why I was so upset? Weren't you hurt, Sean? He's your best friend."

"I felt hurt for a millisecond before that hurt turned into happiness for someone I view as a brother. Why couldn't you just be happy for him? When are you going to get it that he doesn't love you? He never has loved you in the way that you want him to."

I cast my eyes downward to disguise the hatred I'm feeling for him at this moment for reminding me how Cal doesn't want me. His words are like knife slashes to my heart. I realize this would be the best time to start crying. I dig my nails into my thighs underneath the table until tears sting my eyes and look back up at him. The trick works as he leans back in shock, not prepared to see an emotional Cora.

"I *am* realizing that Cal has never loved me in the way he loves Jenna, Sean. Doesn't mean that it doesn't hurt any less. Some of the most important men in my life wouldn't love me the way that I wanted them to. I'm seeing for the first time that my issues from childhood are affecting my behavior." I pinch my leg some more as tears start streaming down my face. "Obviously, I chose the wrong man to love and I'm so sorry for hurting you like I have. Please don't feel like I've never noticed how you've always taken care of me and protected me. I'm sorry I never appreciated you for that." He looks down at his hands, his face softening with my words and that is all the encouragement I need to continue. "You've been a true gentleman and friend to me, Sean. The only one who has ever been there for me and for that, I am forever grateful for."

The waitress comes by to take our order. We both decline food, instead asking for coffee. I take a sip of my water to clear the dryness of my throat before proceeding. "After last night, I can recognize that my anger issues are beyond my control. I need professional help. So I'm going back to London and will be checking into a treatment facility. Philip is working on the details for me as we speak."

He looks at me in stunned silence, his mouth partly open in surprise. He waits for the waitress to put down our coffees before responding. "Philip is helping you with this?"

"Yes, he was happy to help. With him being my agent, he needs to know at all times where I am and what my schedule will be, so it made sense for me to reach out to him for help."

"Wow, Cora. I don't know what to say. I'm … I'm proud of you for doing this." His words make me smile on the inside, but I know this performance is not over yet.

"Thank you, Sean. That means a lot to me." I mentally count to five before continuing on. "Please don't give up on me." I'm getting so good at this that I don't need to pinch myself again in order to cry on command. "I have already lost Cal's friendship.

If I lose yours, I don't think life would be worth living anymore."

"Cora, don't talk like that." Anger flashes in his eyes and he slaps his hands down on the table. For a brief moment, I hope I didn't go too far with that implication.

"It's true, Sean. I have no one in my life anymore. My mother hates me and only uses me for my money, saying I owe her from what she has spent on me as a child. I have no women friends because they all become jealous of me and I have no partner in my life due to wasting my feelings on Cal. I was so blind that I threw away the love from a good man." I pause for my words to sink in for him. "What's the point of living, Sean? My life is fucking miserable," I bitterly say and although this is a performance, I know there's some truth to my words as I *am* miserable. But I've been a fighter all my life and I won't give up until I go down in flames.

I have one last tear left in my eyes, so I grab his hands and squeeze them. "Please Sean, please don't write me off." And the last tears fall on my cheek, perfectly on cue. I stare intently at him, willing him to believe me. He's got to believe me.

You're my last hope.

He reaches across the table and uses the pad of his thumb to wipe away my tears. He keeps his hand on my cheek and caresses it. I close my eyes and relish the touch of his warm hand.

"You haven't lost me, Cora. I will always be your friend."

The audience inside of me jumps up, giving me a standing ovation for my performance. I bite the inside of my cheek to keep from smiling. I cover his hand on my cheek and squeeze it. "Thank you, Sean. You won't regret staying my friend."

He removes his hand, takes a big gulp of his coffee, and lets out a deep sigh. "So, what's the next step?"

"I go home and start working on myself. As soon as Philip secures the treatment facility, I will check in that same day. I have no movies or endorsements lined up, just the press tour, so this is the perfect opportunity to work on me. You know how this industry can eat you up alive. I think this is a wakeup call for me to get back to basics, get back to myself, and everything else will align." I take a sip of my coffee to wash down my bullshit. The waitress puts the check on the table and Sean reaches into his pocket to pull out cash to pay for our bill. I thank him for the coffee and his only response is a nod, clearly at loss for words. He looks at his watch and decides that it is time to go.

"C'mon, I will drive you back to your hotel," he offers and moves out of the booth to leave.

"Thanks, but I think I want to walk. It's a beautiful day and the fresh air would be good for me." I can't have him going to the hotel with me and risk him wanting to escort me to my room since I don't have a room anymore. Sometimes Sean is too much of a gentleman, always making sure people are safe, as if I might be kidnapped from the entrance of the hotel to my room.

"Okay, but why don't I walk with you?" he suggests as we make our way out of the restaurant.

Thank you, Sean, for being so fucking predictable.

"Thanks, but I really want to be alone right now." I move to hug him, squeezing him as tight as I can so he can feel my appreciation. I release him and turn to go, but quickly turn back to him with one last question. "Hey Sean, can I call or text you during my free time in treatment? I know I'm going to need some moral support during the tough times that therapy is going to bring out." I give him a pathetic, sad smile, one that I hope portrays me looking pained.

"Of course you can, Cora. I look forward to hearing of your progress." As soon as the words are out of his mouth, I move quickly to kiss him on the cheek.

"Talk soon, Sean." I turn on my heel and don't look back at him, telling myself to keep the solemn looking facade up until I reach the hotel. Once I see the sign for the hotel, I turn around to look to see if he followed me. When I see that he didn't, I walk past the hotel, hail a cab, and go back to my apartment.

I let out a sigh of relief as soon as I enter my place and lock my door. A celebration is in order and I get out my last bottle of wine from the refrigerator. *Might as well drink it all today so that it doesn't go to waste!* I pour myself a very large glass and sit down on my couch, excited at the idea of not having to look at this shitty view of Lake Michigan anymore.

The next step in my plan is to survive the treatment facility that Philip picks out for me. If I can survive having to turn favors for movie roles, I can survive being psycho analyzed by boring doctors. I already know everything I need to say in order to secure my success in treatment. In the meantime, I need a plan to win Cal back into my life. I have no doubt Sean is going to tell Cal all about our conversation today and they will probably call Philip to verify that he's actually helping me. I smile as I lean back and take a big sip of my wine.

Victory has never tasted so good.

Seventeen

Isla

"YOU'VE GOT TO help me figure out what to do, Robert!" I whine in panic, while I sit across from him on the couch, holding my cup of coffee.

As soon as Sean went into the shower, I bolted from his room in embarrassment, needing to get away from him to think. I went to my room, showered, got dressed, and drove downtown to Robert's apartment. He wasn't very receptive to my presence at such an early hour considering he was tired and hungover from the wedding, but I had nowhere else to go.

"You've got to stop talking to me until I finish my cup of coffee," he groans, holding his head with one of his hands. "I will never let you into my house before ten a.m. on a Sunday ever again." He threatens and I can't help but laugh at his grumpiness.

He takes a sip of his coffee and then rubs his eyes with his free hand. "Okay, tell me again why you ran out of Sean Lindsey's bed, because right now I'm thinking you are bat-shit crazy."

"Because he's going to break my heart," I say, looking at him seriously.

"One night of sex and you're that attached?" He looks at me incredulously, like I am the pathetic little fool that I feel like right about now.

"We haven't even had sex … just oral sex," I clarify, blushing from embarrassment at the memory from this morning. I wasn't planning on revealing that information to Robert, but I didn't want him to think I was a little tart for sleeping with Sean right away either.

"He must give some amazing oral sex for you to have a premonition of him breaking your heart." He raises his eyebrow at me, itching for me to give him the full details of this morning. No one has ever made me come that hard and fast from their mouth. I don't even want to think about how Sean got so talented with his tongue.

"Robert, I don't want to be the rebound girl."

"Technically, you wouldn't be since he and Cora were never officially dating." I roll my eyes at his technicality since he knows exactly what I mean. "But honestly, Izzy, I think he's getting over her. I see the way he looks at you and it's completely different compared to how he looks at Cora."

"Yeah, he looks at me like his play toy and Cora as his forever." I pout, wishing for once that Sean was not back in my life.

Liar.

"Iz, you're sounding like an annoying little girl with a high school crush. You're an adult, who should be able to handle a little oral sex now and again. Let's just rip the Band-Aid off, shall we? You're still in love with him. You don't want to be, but you are. Your heart wants him, and so does your vagina, so why don't you satisfy both organs by seeing where this goes?" I start choking on my coffee from the shock of his bluntness. Jenna warned me that Robert is into tough love, but I was not prepared to be slapped with it so early in the morning.

"Oh, my God, I think you made me just get coffee up my nose," I wheeze out in between coughs. I get up from the couch to get a tissue before I get coffee snot everywhere.

"Why does this all of a sudden feel like déjà vu?" Robert playfully looks up to the sky while tapping his index finger to his lips. "Oh, I know! Because I had the same freaking conversation years ago with Jenna when Cal came into her life and look where they are now."

"Cal is completely different from Sean," I counter back, the situations being vastly different with zero comparison.

"No shit," Robert says sarcastically. "Cal was never in love with a sociopath. But guess what, I don't think Sean is either. I think he has always been enamored with the idea of being her knight in shining armor, saving Cora from her miserable life and hoping they live happily ever after. Despite Cora's beauty, because let's be honest, she *is* beautiful, she's rotten to the core and will never change. I think Sean sees what his best friend has and is starting to want that for himself."

I listen carefully to Robert's words, wishing they didn't make as much sense as they do, because it makes me have sympathy for Sean and his good intentions that were never rewarded by the one person he wanted.

"You wouldn't be his rebound, Isla. You might be the woman who teaches him what true love is really supposed to be about. Do you think you're up for that challenge?"

"That challenge comes with a huge risk, one that I don't know if I'm willing to take just yet," I whisper as I sit down next to him. I'm past the point of staying away from Sean and if I feel this way just from oral sex with him, I'm going to be a complete goner once we do have sex. I'm not strong enough to deny him, and I want him just as badly as he seems to want me. But am I willing to risk my heart just to be tossed aside once it's time for him to leave in a month?

"Love is a risk, Izzy. If you want to be loved, then you have to take that risk. Otherwise, you'll live with regret."

God, he's right. I have been telling myself that I need to live life without regrets and I know that if I don't take that leap with Sean, it would be one of the biggest regrets in my life.

"He wants to take me to dinner tonight and discuss how his meeting with Cora went today. That's the thing though, is he always going to be at her beck and call? Because I don't know if

I can handle that." I don't care how long they have been friends for. If Sean puts Cora first, then that's a deal breaker.

"Wait, hold up. Sean asked you out on a date *and* he's meeting with Cora today? That's some very important information that you have left out, young lady!" Robert rubs his hands together, his eyes taking an evil shine to them. "I hope he's ripping her a new one for her behavior last night. Knowing him, he probably isn't, although I did get a glimpse of him when he was sitting with her and he looked fierce. I took note never to get on his bad side. What time are you meeting him tonight?"

"I don't know, I haven't responded back yet." I give him a sheepish grin, knowing he is going to yell at me for not already responding back with a yes.

Just as I predict, he rolls his eyes at me and throws his hands up in exasperation. "What is wrong with you? A big time Hollywood actor has asked you out and you haven't responded yet?"

"He's not a big time Hollywood actor to me. In fact, I want no part of that life." I shake my head in disgust, hating that fame has to come with his job. I always get nervous when I'm out with Jenna and Cal and the paparazzi stalk us. Even the crazy fans that come up to Cal make me uncomfortable. No amount of money is worth that invasion of privacy to me.

"Okay, Jenna from years past, keep dreaming of a life without the man you love. See where that gets you. In the meantime, confirm with Sean that you will go out with him so we can find out where he's taking you." He points his finger at my phone, waiting to watch me send Sean a text. I stick my tongue out at him and comply.

"Let's go get breakfast and then go shopping. I'll go wake up sleeping beauty." Robert gets up to go into his bedroom to wake up Kellan, but stops short when we hear shouting coming from the room.

"Sleeping Beauty is awake because you two can wake up the dead with those loud ass voices!" Kellan walks out of the room, only wearing his boxer shorts, his beautiful dark skin contrasting against the whiteness of his shorts. He gives Robert a kiss and heads straight for the coffee maker. "You better be treating us to a hearty breakfast this morning, Isla, because we're going to need all the energy to speed shop for something fabulous in order to get you ready for tonight."

"You're going to go shopping with us?" I inquire in excitement, because I've never been styled by a professional stylist before.

"Of course, I am! I can never say no to getting Cinderella ready for her ball." He winks at me and I squeal with glee as I hug him. He sticks his finger in his ear and wiggles it to try to regain his hearing that he has seemed to have lost from my sharp pitched tone. "Just promise me you'll never do that around Sean ever in your lifetime."

I SIT NERVOUSLY in my car in the parking lot of the restaurant, taking one last look at my appearance before getting out to meet Sean.

I had the best time shopping with Robert and Kellan today. While I have been shopping with Robert before, shopping with Kellan is a whole other experience. Because of who he is in the industry, we were escorted to all of the private rooms, having our very own personal shopper at our disposal with rows and rows of outfits picked out specifically for me. Sean sent me the place and time of our destination and we looked it up online to see that it's a trendy Asian fusion restaurant downtown. Once we found the perfect dress and shoes, Kellan arranged for my hair and makeup to be professionally done while he picked out some jewelry. After seeing the brands he was looking at, I was adamant that he stop due to how expensive everything was getting. He told me to relax and not worry since he has it all taken care of, which makes me quite suspicious as to who is really footing the bill for my outfit.

I take a deep breath and exit my car, grateful that there was a parking lot exactly next door to the restaurant so that I didn't have to walk far in these heels. I can already see that Sean is waiting outside for me by the amount of flashing light bulbs from the paparazzi taking his photo. Despite dusk settling onto the early evening sky, Sean wears his sunglasses to help protect him from the glare of the flashing lights. He looks between the paparazzi and sees me walking toward him. He moves past them and reaches for my hand, leading me in silence to the restaurant. I cast my eyes downward and avoid answering the questions that are coming from them of why Cal Harrington's nanny is having dinner with Sean Lindsey.

Once inside the safety of the restaurant, Sean takes off his sunglasses, confirms our reservation with the hostess, and turns his full attention on admiring me from head to toe. I see the heat light up his eyes and I can't help clenching my thighs together as the sight of him overtakes me.

"You look stunning," he murmurs into my ear and kisses my cheek. I feel like he branded me with the heat that's coming off of his soft lips. *I want those lips for dessert*, and with the way he is looking at me, dessert is definitely in my future for tonight.

As the hostess leads us to our table in the back of the restaurant, I can feel the buzz of chatter in the air of people recognizing him. All eyes are upon us and even some cell phones are out with people taking videos. That uncomfortable feeling starts to arise, but I try to squash it when I'm seated across from Sean. He takes off his brown leather jacket and drapes it around his chair, giving me the opportunity to appreciate how his black button-down shirt molds to his muscular arms, the top two buttons opened enough to give me a peekaboo viewing of the top of his chest. My eyes make their way back up to his, where I see a devilish smile play on his lips as he caught me checking him out.

"With the rate that we're going, this will be the fastest dinner date in history. I can't wait to get you in the privacy of my room."

He gives me one more searing look with his eyes before turning his attention to the drink menu. "What would you like to drink?"

"Wine, please." *And lots of it!* I have no plans on getting drunk, but wine is needed to take the edge off of my nerves. We order a bottle of white wine and a couple of appetizers to share.

"Before I ask how your day was, I'm dying to know why you took off so quickly this morning after we had such an amazing experience together."

My eyes go wide since I was not expecting that to be the first thing he asks me, but what's most shocking is for him to think giving me oral sex was an amazing experience for him.

"I'm sorry," I stammer as my cheeks heat up in mortification. "I um …well, I've never experienced such an intense orgasm from someone's mouth before and it made me embarrassed by how I reacted to it." I nervously laugh and take a big sip of my wine that the waitress just put down on the table. As soon as she leaves, Sean leans closer toward me, his eyes intense with longing.

"Don't ever be ashamed of your reaction. It made me harder than I already was with anticipation of when I finally get to be inside of you."

His words just destroyed my panties.

"Keep looking at me like that, Isla, and we'll be taking a trip to the restroom together." I watch as his hand disappears underneath the table to adjust himself and snap my gaze back up to his eyes in realization of why it went down there in the first place.

"I'm sorry!" I screech a little too loudly, wishing I could be one of those girls who can play cool and be flirty at the same time. Instead, I'm a train wreck of balled up nervousness. I'm not comfortable in this public element when all I want to do is crawl into his lap and hump him.

"Don't ever be sorry for making my dick hard for you." He gives me a wicked grin, leans back, and takes another look at the menu before shutting it closed. "Now that we got that out of the way, tell me how your day was?"

"Oh, it was just another fun day of shopping with Robert. This time Kellan joined us, giving me a sneak peek at what it's like being in your world."

"It can get very pretentious, but also quite accommodating having everything ready and picked out for you. Sometimes I do miss being able to just pop into a mall and go shopping without having to stop and take pictures with fans. But it comes with the territory and I'm very blessed." He smiles politely as the waitress returns to take our order.

"How did your meeting with Cora go?" I inquire as soon as the waitress is out of ear shot. Curiosity has been killing me all day to know what was said between them regarding last night.

"She knows she has fucked up. Cal won't even talk to her. She says she has realized that she has anger issues stemming from childhood and will be seeking treatment for it when she gets home to London."

My mouth drops open in shock as that is the last thing I expected to hear. Cora Gregory has never taken responsibility for any of her previous words or actions. I narrow my eyes at him, doubt creeping in my bones. "Do you really believe her, Sean? That sounds very uncharacteristic of her."

"I don't have any reason not to believe her this time since Philip confirmed that he's looking for the treatment facility for her." He shrugs his shoulders while he swishes his wine around his glass before drinking it. "I honestly think she has hit rock bottom. We'll see how she does when we see her for the press tour."

My stomach starts to feel queasy at the thought of him being alone with her in all of those different cities together. Yes, it's for work and there will be other people around, but that has not stopped Cora in the past from getting what she wants. "When does she go back to London?" I ask nonchalantly, hoping he doesn't hear the hope in my voice at her being far, far away.

"She leaves tomorrow."

We end our discussion on Cora and fill the rest of our evening with easy conversation about the status of our families and stories of our time away from each other in our respective boarding schools. Sean knows how to put you at ease with his charm and funny storytelling. Before I realize it, we've been at the restaurant for three hours and he managed to pay the bill without my knowledge.

"You ready to go home or do you want to go somewhere else for dessert?" He stands up to put his jacket on and all I can think about is how I finally want to taste those lips for myself.

"I think I want dessert at the house. Preferably in your room." Three drinks later and apparently my filter got destroyed along with my panties. I laugh at the look of shock that just came over his face. It's nice to know that I can keep him on his toes just as he does with me.

"Let's go," he growls with yearning and grabs my hand to lead us out of the restaurant. As soon as we walk out that door, the paparazzi start taking our photo, blinding us with their flashes.

"Where's your car?" He shouts over the loudness of the paparazzi and their questioning. I point to where it is and give him the keys when he asks for them. He opens my door first to make sure I get in safely before coming around to the driver's side to drive us home. I'm thankful he is driving, because the paparazzi have surrounded my car, the flashes of lights seem to be lighting up the night's sky.

"How do you get used to this?" I question while I cover my eyes while Sean honks the horn and slowly eases into traffic once the paparazzi let us through.

"You don't really. The life of a famous actor is one of a hermit's life. You tend to become a homebody because everything you need can now be delivered to you without having to deal with this every time you need something. It also depends on where you live. Here in the States, it seems to be much worse than back home in Ireland."

This information makes me feel better knowing that it's

not always like this. I can deal with it if it's once in a while, but I wouldn't sacrifice my freedom if this was an everyday occurrence. "Do you think they are following us?" They always follow whenever Jenna and I are downtown together, so I can only imagine that being with Sean would bring out even more photographers.

Sean looks in the rearview mirror a couple of times as he drives and nods. "Yeah, we have a couple of tails, but they can't get into Jenna and Cal's neighborhood and they know that. Once they see we're heading there, they'll turn around."

The rest of the drive is in compatible silence, with Sean grabbing my hand and holding it while we cruise on the highway. I look down at our entwined hands, admiring how long and strong his fingers are. Those same fingers that were inside of me this morning. I squeeze my legs together and the movement grabs Sean's attention. He looks down at my legs briefly and nestles our joined hands right on the top of my mound. He frees his pinky from my grasp and starts to rub against me. I open my legs wider and scoot down into the car seat for him to have better access. I grip his hands tighter when I feel he has connected with my bud through the layers of my dress. As he starts to rub harder, his slow motion precisely hitting its mark, I loudly moan out as pleasure starts to mount within me.

"That's my girl," he purrs as he flicks the turn signal on, indicating we are getting off the highway. "I can't wait to taste you again."

Not thinking that it's fair that he's doing all the work, I place my hand on his groin and feel it stiffen underneath my touch. I start to rub, pressing my fingers against the fabric of his jeans so he can feel the friction. It continues to grow underneath my touch, making my eyes water with need of him to be inside me.

"Isla," he groans out, his breath starting to hitch as I increase the speed of my hand on him. "You need to stop or we might get into an accident. We're almost home." I see that he's right since I recognize the street we just passed. I pout and remove my hand from his erection in disappointment.

A few minutes later, we pull up to the guard gate at the front of the community entrance. He untangles his hand from mine to retrieve his ID from his wallet. As soon as we're cleared, he speeds down the street to the house and punches the gate code in when we arrive. Once we've pulled through the gates and parked the car, Sean then turns off the engine and looks at me.

Without another word, we reach for each other, the need to finally taste what we have been craving all night long too strong to deny any longer. As our mouths touch, our kiss is anything but light and sweet.

It's hungry, primal, and hard.

He slips his tongue through and I whimper in happiness because he tastes as good as I knew he would. We try to get as close to each other as we possibly can, but the middle console of the car makes it difficult. We finally release each other in order to catch our breaths.

"There's no turning back, Isla, because now that I've had a taste of you, I want more. Promise you'll stop running from me?" His eyes search mine, waiting for me to show any kind of hesitation. I'm done running from him. All I want to do right now is run *into* his arms.

"I promise," I confirm and am rewarded with one of the most breathtaking smiles I've ever seen from him. We give each other a knowing look and get out of the car. He reaches for my hand again once we are within distance of each other and run the rest of the way toward the house, our laughter of excitement for what's to come filling the night air. We quietly let ourselves in and race up the stairs, only to come short at the sound of Brooks crying.

Before we can get to Sean's room, Jenna is in the hallway, trying to shush Brooks when she sees us. She stops and just stares at our entwined hands, then her gaze travels to our attire and then to our faces.

"Hi," she says with an awkward smile. "How are you guys?"

"Fine, but what's wrong with Brooks?" I inquire, reluctantly releasing Sean's hand and walk over to Jenna to help her soothe him.

"I think he had a nightmare. Shook him up real good since he won't stop crying. I was going to take him downstairs so he wouldn't wake up Avery and to see if milk will help calm him down."

As if on cue, Avery's door opens and she comes out with disheveled hair, rubbing her eyes from sleep. "Mommy, why won't Brooksy stop crying?" She removes her fists from her eyes and upon seeing three adults, her eyes become wide with excitement. "Uncle Sean!" She runs to him and he picks her up to nestle her against his hip.

"Wow Izzy, you look so pretty," she says, her eyes looking over my dress. "Did you go out on a date with a boy looking like that?"

I laugh at her astuteness, especially since the 'boy' is the one holding her. "I sure did." I wink at Sean, who wiggles his eyebrows up and down at me.

"Avery, you need to go back to bed," Jenna tells her while trying to soothe Brooks.

"But I want someone to put me to bed. I can't go back to sleep now with Brooksy being so loud. His screams hurt my ears." Avery turns her attention to me, her blue eyes looking like a little lost puppy who wants some attention. "Izzy, will you put me to sleep?"

I look at Sean and he smiles at me, understanding that this probably means the end to our night. With a slight nod, he puts Avery down when I agree to put her to bed.

"Thank you, Isla," Jenna says and then proceeds to mouth out, "I'm so sorry!"

"It's okay. C'mon, Avery." With one last look of longing at Sean, I grab Avery's hand and escort her back to bed.

As I lay down next to her and rub her back to soothe her to sleep, I can't help the smile that stays permanently on my face from my night with Sean. I sigh in contentment, happy that I took Robert's advice because tonight was the perfect first date.

And I look forward to many more perfect evenings with Sean to come.

Eighteen

Sean

IF I DIDN'T know any better, I would've thought the Harrington children were conspiring against their dear ol' Uncle Sean with the way they have been blue balling me from Isla during our vacation. I understood I wasn't going to get to have alone time with Isla on the first night of our arrival due to everyone's exhaustion from such an exciting first day. Avery's reaction when she figured out where we were going was priceless and in no time, she had us running ragged around the Magic Kingdom. Jenna arranged for a special tour guide, so we were able to hit every single ride and meet every single princess imaginable within an eight-hour timeframe. After a long day at the park, we checked into a mammoth rental home Jenna found, located in a gated community with its own private pool, tennis courts, and playground. The house is able to fit all of us, but since I was the last-minute addition, I had to sleep on the third twin bed inside the room that houses the younger male Harrington cousins. Jenna did nothing to hide her glee when she was showing me where my sleeping accommodations were. She and Cal decided to sleep at a hotel near the airport because their flight out the next day was very early. Isla was sleeping in a room with Brooks and Avery. I didn't think the sleeping arrangements were going to prevent me from getting alone time with Isla since the kids go to bed usually before we do.

Boy, did they have me fooled!

Those little buggers, along with their cousins, stayed up until midnight every single night that we've been here. What makes it even worse is that Avery and Brooks seem even more attached to Isla since their parents aren't around, despite having their grandparents, aunts, uncles, and cousins here from England to spend time with them.

The week has gone quickly and I can't handle not being able to touch Isla any longer. Just staring at her lush lips and wondering what they would look like around my cock has made me take multiple showers a day. *Enough is enough!* Tonight is our last night here before Cal and Jenna arrive tomorrow and I have a plan in motion.

I decide to forego visiting Disney again with the rest of the family in order to conduct business with Philip and meet with my assistant since they are both based here in California. I killed two birds with one stone by having a lunch meeting with both of them, signing off on a new movie contract that will start to shoot next year and finalizing travel and itinerary plans for the upcoming press tour. While meeting with my assistant, I had her book a room for Isla and me at an upscale hotel in the Presidential Suite that's close to the house for tonight. Now I just need to get the Harringtons to agree to watch the kids for us.

I make it back to the house just as everyone is coming back from the park. The children immediately go get their swimsuits on, which gives me an opportunity to ask Cal's sisters if they will watch over Avery and Brooks tonight.

"Why does one of us need to sleep with the children, Sean?" Jane, Cal's oldest sister, asks me with a raised eyebrow. I kept my request pretty vague, which I should've known wouldn't be acceptable considering how nosey those two are.

"Because Isla will not be sleeping here tonight." I give her a sweet smile, hoping she'll take the hint that I don't want to divulge any details in front of the older Harringtons, who just happen to walk into the kitchen to get some snacks for the kids.

Bridget, the second eldest sister, looks over at her parents and then at her sister. The two share some sort of secret message and then look at me with devious grins on their faces.

I'm screwed!

"And where, pray tell, will the sweet, beautiful Isla be sleeping tonight, Sean?" Bridget inquires in a loud voice, batting her eyelashes at me with a wicked smile. These two are like naughty little Siamese twin cats, getting ready to cause mischief. I'm shocked that Cal survived childhood with them as sisters.

"I have decided to treat my new girlfriend to a wonderful night out in a hotel." *There, the cat is out of the bag now.*

"Girlfriend, eh? Funny how Cal and Jenna never mentioned that you and their nanny are dating. When did that come about?" Cal's father has now joined the conversation and I can already feel my body start to sweat underneath his stare. Cal definitely gets his intensity from his dad, just not as severe. I used to loathe getting into trouble at Cal's house when we were younger, because just the thought of receiving one death stare from Charles Harrington was all it took to scare me. My parents were too busy to punish me for getting into trouble, but not Cal's dad. He had no problems handing out punishments to children who misbehaved in his home.

"We are newly dating, sir. Trying to keep it quiet from Avery so she doesn't worry that I might take Isla away from her."

"Will you take Isla away from her? Because if you want this relationship to go somewhere, then she can't be their nanny forever now, can she? She'll be with you, won't she?" I swallow the ball of anxiety that has formed from his rapid-fire inquisition and smile at him, hoping my charm will yet again save me from my uncomfortableness.

"I haven't thought that far out yet, sir. Just seeing if we are compatible and living in the moment." My shoulders sag with relief when Isla and the children walk in, rescuing me from any more questions. Avery runs toward me and wraps her little arms around my waist in a hug. Isla comes to stand next to me with Brooks.

"Isla, we are going to watch the kids for you tonight so you can have some quality time with your *boyfriend*," Charles announces while looking me up and down in warning before grabbing a beer and heading outside to the pool. Isla gives me a funny look, while Cal's sisters try to hide their giggling.

"Eew, you have a boyfriend, Izzy? Don't you know boys are gross?" Avery scrunches up her cute little nose while still holding onto me. "Their breath smells and they eat boogers."

"How did you know that your Uncle Sean eats his boogers, Avery?" I shoot daggers at Bridget, hoping Avery doesn't put two and two together now.

"Uncle Sean is your boyfriend?" Avery shrieks as she drops her arms from around my waist and looks between the both of us in denial.

"Wow, one date and you think I'm your girlfriend already? *Creep-y*!" Isla leans in close and jokes softly, mischief gleaming from her sexy eyes.

"You can't be her boyfriend, Uncle Sean! You don't live with us and Isla can't leave us!" Tears start to form in Avery's eyes and I start to panic since I can't handle Avery upset. She definitely has me wrapped around her gorgeous little finger. "Please don't take her away from me," she whimpers, robbing me of speech as I look at Isla for help.

Isla kneels down to her eye level and gives her a hug. "Avery, your Uncle Sean is not taking me away from you."

"Well, only for tonight I am." Isla's head shoots up in surprise at my announcement. "Sorry, but I wanted to ask the Harringtons if they would watch the kids first before telling you." I get down on my knees in front of Avery and look into her stormy blue eyes. "I promise she will be here in the morning."

Avery sniffs and looks at Isla, who gives her an encouraging smile, before looking back at me. "Okay, but you better be nice to her or I won't love you anymore!" Avery stomps her feet and gives me her own little death stare that she inherited from her father's side. Before I can reassure her, screams of laughter from the pool catch her attention and she races out there to be part of it.

"Can you please go pack a bag so we can leave before Brooks decides he's going to start talking at one and questions me as well?" Isla throws her head back in laughter, hands Brooks to Jane, and runs to go pack a bag.

I thank everyone and remove myself to wait in the car for Isla before Cal's family decides to continue their fun at my expense.

"Wow, THIS PLACE is beautiful!" Isla exclaims as we enter the hotel suite an hour later. She walks ahead of me, her mouth open in awe at the beautiful decor of the full-size kitchen and living room. She looks and stares over at the ceiling-to-floor windows to admire the view we have from being at the top of the hotel. My eyes are transfixed on her, marveling at the fact of how beautiful she looks in a simple black sundress with her hair down and minimal makeup on. The scent of food hits my senses, reminding me that I ordered room service to be waiting for us when we arrived. My stomach grumbles at the delicious smell and I concede to the fact that I might have to wait a little bit longer to make Isla mine.

Isla inhales the scent of food as well, looking at me in question before walking over toward the dining room to see a table set for two with cover plates of food, wine, and a bouquet of roses. I walk over to where she is standing and wrap my arms around her from behind, pulling her against my chest.

"You did all of this for me?" she whispers, as she turns her head to look at me, gratitude shining in her eyes.

"Selfishly, I did it for us because I couldn't take another night not being able to touch you."

She turns around in my arms and caresses my cheek. With our eyes locked on each other's lips, she slowly moves her head toward mine and kisses me. Softly at first, each kiss being more of a sensual peck of glorious torture, as if she is studying the shape and firmness of my lips. Her kisses start to linger longer and before long, she slips her tongue past my lips, making me moan with happiness at finally getting to taste her. Her hands make their way into my hair, gripping me closer to her as our tongues continue tangling together. She's making me delirious with the need to be inside of her and soon my hand makes its way down her back, grabbing her ass to crush her pelvis to mine so she can feel how hard I am for her.

She slows our kisses down, removing her tongue from mine and steps back. She gives me a slow, salacious smile while grabbing my hand and leading me to the bedroom. This confident, take-charge side of Isla is the sexiest thing I have ever seen, making my erection scream for immediate release out of my pants.

"Don't you want to eat first?" I ask hoarsely, still trying to be somewhat of a gentleman, when all I want to do is completely ravish her. She takes us straight into the bedroom and to my utter surprise, starts taking off her clothes.

"Food can wait, Sean. I've got to have you inside me now." She pulls off her dress and the sight of her in only her black lace bra and thong almost makes me come undone. I close my eyes, imbedding that image into my brain forever and when I open them back up, she is standing in front of me, working the buttons of my shirt free with her magical fingers. Once all the buttons are done, she pushes the shirt down my arms and throws it to the floor. I place my hands on the curve of her hips and start kissing her neck as her hands unbuckle my belt, pulling it out of the loopholes of my jeans. My tongue makes a trail of hot kisses down her neck and clavicle, my fingers unhooking her bra behind her back. Once her breasts are free, I descend upon one of her nipples, her moans of pleasure making my cock ache with need. I continue my assault on her breasts as I guide her with my hands to walk backwards until the back of her legs hit the end of the bed. I release my hold on her nipple, stand to my full height and look deep into her eyes, silently communicating to her that once she's on that bed, she is going to be mine.

As if she understands exactly what I'm thinking, she sits down on the bed, looks up at me and continues taking off my pants, her eyes never wavering from mine. She pushes my pants and underwear down to my ankles and stares at my cock that is begging for her touch. I expect her eyes to be fearful when her gaze comes back up to mine.

Instead, it is full of hunger.

She licks her lips before wrapping her soft hands around my shaft, squeezing it slowly while she rubs her thumb against the head, rubbing the pre-cum that has surfaced. I inhale sharply as she slowly smiles before guiding me into her mouth. Her lips close around me and I feel like I'm going to come right then when I feel her tongue lapping me up.

"Fuck, that's hot," I hiss as I watch her slowly move her mouth up and down my cock. I thrust my hands into her head and start massaging her, guiding her a little faster. She moans at the increased tempo and wraps her arms around me, her hands squeezing my ass while she sucks me harder. My hips start moving faster against her mouth and it won't be long before I am done. This is not how I want our first night of sex to be together, so I slow myself down and put my hands on her shoulders, squeezing them to get her attention.

"Lie back," I command and her eyes light up when she realizes what is about to happen. She releases me from her mouth and lies down. I get down on my knees in front of her, grab the sides of her thong, and bring it down her legs and feet, throwing it to the floor with my shirt. I start kissing the insides of her thigh to get her to open them wider for me. My tongue starts to make love to her clit, her moans purring loudly as I bring her higher and higher to ecstasy. When I feel her getting close, I release her and grab my pants to get the condoms out of my pocket.

As soon as I roll one on, I stand up and align my cock with her opening. I take the tip of it and bring it to her clit, slowly rubbing my head up and down, teasing her until she is panting for more.

"Please get inside me, Sean, please!" she begs and I love hearing my name come out of her mouth. I pull her legs closer, causing her hips to come slightly off the bed. I hold them straight up as I enter her slowly, both of us groaning at how amazing it feels. I grit my teeth at how tight she is, feeling her walls gripping me already. I'm not going to last long if she keeps doing that. I slowly start moving in and out of her, relishing in the feeling of finally being inside of her. I lick the pad of my thumb and bring it to her bud, rubbing back and forth as I move faster inside of her. Her hands are at her sides, fisting the sheets. Her moans coming out faster while I rub her harder, trying to be in sync with the rhythm of my pelvis. Her eyes are closed, mouth open, and suddenly I feel her squeezing me tighter. Her eyes snap open to mine and she screams out her orgasm, her reaction making me roar out my own release at the exact same time. I fall over her, my arms bracing me so I don't crush her as I thrust the remnants of my release. Her hands grip my ass as she tightens a couple more times around me and then stops. I relieve my arms and lay on top of her, her legs still wrapped around me. We struggle to catch our breaths while we slowly come down from the most amazing high I've ever experienced. I feel her heart rapidly beating and know that she couldn't have faked what just transpired between us.

I roll to my side to avoid crushing her, wrapping my arms around her so that we can cuddle side-by-side together. As I brush the hair out of her face, her eyes slowly open, shining with love.

I should be scared by the sight of it, but instead, I bask in it, hoping I'm not too damaged enough to love her back.

Nineteen

Cora

IT HAS BEEN one week since I checked into this hell hole of a treatment facility, with one more week of added torture to endure. The first week they took away our cell phones and computers in order for us not to have any contact with the outside world. They wanted us to focus on intense therapy, identifying the root of our anger and what outside, unrelated forces, trigger it.

I feel my anger is pretty self-explanatory once you hear my case.

I was abandoned by my father.

My mother hates me and uses me for money.

The man I want is in love—and now married—to someone else.

The one man I could've had, I pushed away and now doesn't seem to want me either.

I have no friends who care about me.

No one in my industry takes me seriously.

To sum it up, my life is pretty fucking depressing.

This week, we are supposed to focus on how to handle each situation when our anger is triggered and focus on what makes us happy.

A life with Cal Harrington is the only thing that would make me happy.

I wait in line to get my cell phone since today is the first day that we're allowed to have them back. I bum a cigarette from another attendee, grab my phone when my turn is up, and walk outside to hear my messages. I wait with anticipation as I turn my phone back on, a smile playing on my lips knowing that there will be numerous missed texts and phone calls.

But reality comes crashing down as I see I only had one missed call and one text. Both from my agent, Philip.

Not one call or text from my mother.

Not one call or text from Cal.

Not even a call or text from Sean.

Disappointment and rage fill me with the realization that no one cares about how I'm doing here. I take a couple of deep long breaths and call Philip back.

"Cora! How are you?" Philip asks, sounding genuinely sincere. Of course he cares about me–I make him money. "I was getting worried about you when I hadn't heard from you, so I called the facility and they explained that you weren't allowed to have your phone."

Knowing that he checked up on me brightens my mood somewhat. I force myself to smile and make my voice softer so he thinks I'm in a state of calmness.

"Philip, I'm so good. This place has been amazing so far. How are you doing? Thank you for checking in on me." I pretend I'm one of those Stepford wives, my voice monotoned and pleasant all in one.

"Of course I was going to check in on you. I've got some great news for you!" He adds with excitement, making my heart speed up at the hopes it's a new endorsement deal. "I received a phone call two days ago from the office of His Royal Highness, Prince Khalid Rashid al-Hamad. He is requesting your presence at one of his lavish state dinners next month in Qatar."

My smile falters as this was *not* the news I was expecting. "Why is this good news and why would I even consider attending?" I question, wondering if Philip has lost his damn mind. I've heard of some Hollywood actresses being offered an all-expense paid trip to the wealthy countries of the Middle East in exchange for the publicity. Some of them come back happy, some of them haven't come back at all.

"The good news is that this Prince is quite handsome and photos together would gain a lot of attention. The reason why you would even consider this is that he's offering you a million dollars for your appearance." I inhale sharply, shocked at such a large sum for just showing up to take some photos. Skepticism creeps in as this sounds almost too good to be true.

"I don't know about this, Philip. How long would I have to be there and what do they want me to do?"

"It would only be for three days and there are various parties he would like you to attend as his date. I researched him, and not only is he handsome, but has a reputation of being fair and mild mannered compared to his older siblings. I will send over to you what I found, along with photos of him. They want a decision made within forty-eight hours though."

"Why so quickly?" I wonder, the thought of traveling to the Middle East by myself unsettling me.

"They want time to be able to talk to other actresses if you turn them down." His answer makes sense and I agree to think about it since my financially situation is pretty dire right now.

"Any other news? Any movies or new endorsements? Television deals?"

"Unfortunately, not yet. I'm trying though. Had a good meeting with one of the big studios last week and put some visions in their head that included you as their lead for the future movies they have lined up." He goes silent for a split second and I can tell another call is coming in. "Oh hey, I need to take this call that is coming in. Call me when you have made your decision." He hangs up on me before I can say goodbye. I will give his offer some thought after I do a little investigating of my own.

Speaking of investigating, I call Danny Salari next to find out what new information he has for me from his week of spying on Cal and Sean.

He greets me as if he's already bored talking to me, not even asking me how I'm feeling. "Tell me something that's going to make me happy, Danny," I purr, deciding to be nice to him for once. Maybe I can even muster up some gratitude for him doing so much of my dirty work for me.

"Well, don't have much on Cal since he just got back from screwing his new wife's brains out in Bora Bora all last week. Sean Lindsey keeps being photographed out with their nanny. Looks like they are dating as they've been seen holding hands and kissing."

"I told you I wanted happy fucking news, not news that's going to make me want to slit my wrists!" I scream into the phone, my blood pressure now through the roof after hearing this news.

"If you want happy news, keep your phone off then, because there's nothing I got that you're going to like since you want to destroy other people's happiness," he says matter-of-factly, making me wish I never called him in the first place.

"Fuck you, Salari! Keep those threats going to Jenna and make sure you're ready for our trip to Europe in two weeks." I hang up and throw my phone as hard as I can into the grass, wishing it would shatter into a thousand pieces since nothing good came out of it today.

I start to pace, needing my nerves to calm down so I can think of what I need to do next. After a couple of minutes, I pick up my phone, sit down on a bench, and take a couple of deep breaths to get myself under control before I have to report back inside. I only have one week left here and then another week left to prepare for the press tour. I take one last big inhale of my cigarette and stub it out on the ground.

It's time, for once, to make myself happy.

Winning Cal Harrington is going to be the only thing that brings happiness back into my life.

It's time to get serious and prepare how to make that happen.

Just the thought of having something to scheme makes me smile, and I get up and go back in for lunch.

Who says it doesn't feel good to be bad?

Twenty

Isla

I'M SITTING WITH Jenna in her bedroom, trying to help her pack up the children's suitcases since we start our journey to London tomorrow for the press tour. The past three weeks have been a blur with my days occupied with the children, while my nights are occupied by Sean and his sinful mouth and addictive body. He has completely consumed me, heart and soul, making me happier than I've ever been.

It has been a dream, one that I don't want to wake up from.

A dream that I'm scared will be crushed once we see Cora Gregory again.

I know he has been in communication with her because his face changes every time he reads a message from her. She's constantly texting him and every time he smiles at something she says, a new crack forms in my heart. Even though his attention is only diverted by her for a short amount of time, it's enough for her to weasel her way back into his heart.

My head tried to warn my heart that this might happen and as each ticking second gets closer to that press tour, dread starts pouring in, whispering that he might not be mine to keep. That I need to be able to walk away if he decides he wants her instead of me.

I haven't told him that I love him, but I know he can see it in my eyes. I don't expect to hear those words from him yet, but each moment we spend together, each moment that he's inside me, is another moment that I fall harder for him. I wish I could say that I trust in us, but without confirmation that his heart is mine, I fear we are too fragile to withstand the destruction that Cora is bound to unleash.

"Earth to Isla, are you listening to me?" I snap my attention back to Jenna, who's looking at me with a bemused smile. "You okay, over there? You look like you were having an argument with yourself."

"Sorry, just have a lot on mind," I tell her with a smile. Although Jenna knows exactly the kind of person Cora is, she didn't have to deal with the uncertainty of Cal's feelings for her.

"Are you just feeling overwhelmed by attending the premiere with Sean?" I felt mixed emotions when Sean asked me to be his date. Excitement that he wanted me there with him on his big day, but apprehension at being in close proximity to Cora. Fortunately, Jenna will be there with Cal and was actually happy that Sean asked me to go. She made arrangements for Cal's family to watch the kids and her and I had our final dress fittings with Kellan last week. Sean asked me to be his date for the rest of the premieres, but I told him I didn't want to overstep my bounds by asking for too much time off, especially since I will be spending my week off in Ireland with him once the European leg of the press tour is over with.

"Something like that. I honestly have no idea what to expect and am getting nervous about it." I smile politely and continue helping her fold clothes into the suitcase.

"Is this really about the premiere or is there something else?" She gives me a look of understanding and I can't hold back my dam of emotions any longer.

"I don't have a good feeling about Cora being around." I look down and fiddle with Avery's sock, not wanting Jenna to see the tears in my eyes. "I don't know why I'm feeling this way. Sean hasn't given me any reasons to be worried about."

"Oh Isla," she sighs and puts down Brooks' pants to squeeze my hand. "You're in a new relationship with someone who is internationally famous. It's a world much bigger than you and I could ever dream about. You are feeling insecure and with the past history between Sean and Cora, I can't blame you for feeling that way. I would probably be feeling the same way."

"You would?" I look up at her, a lone tear falling down my cheek. Without hesitation, she takes her index finger and wipes it away, sympathy etched onto her face while she looks in my eyes.

"Stay confident and true to you, Isla. Fight for Sean if you feel he's worth it, but don't let her see you hesitate. If she sees any cracks in your armor, she will come after it and keep picking at it until it's unrepairable." I nod slowly at her in comprehension. She pats my hand and resumes folding Brooks' clothes. "I'm here for you whenever you need to talk, Isla."

I give her a weak smile, taking comfort in knowing that I have her to talk to. I decide to ignore my feelings, telling myself that I'm being ridiculous and to not worry about something that may not even happen. Who knows, maybe Cora is getting better in treatment and that I should be more sympathetic to what she is going through? I believe in second chances and maybe Cora deserves hers.

But some nagging feeling inside me screams to be aware.

***

"Mind if I join you?" I look up from staring into the running water coming out of the facet to see Sean standing in my doorway. I'm not surprised to see him here since we don't hide our relationship from anyone anymore and he comes and goes from my room as he pleases now. I haven't seen much of him today because he was busy preparing for his trip with phone interviews and meetings, so I was eagerly anticipating his attention. But tonight at dinner, when I saw him staring at his phone again, reading something from *her*, I knew I had to get away and be alone with my thoughts. As soon as the kids were done eating, I volunteered to get them ready for bed. Once that was accomplished, I then went straight to my room and decided a nice, relaxing steam bath was in order, hoping it would clear my thoughts away. I didn't get very far in that process when Sean arrived.

"Of course I don't mind." I can't help smiling at his excitement and how quickly he takes his clothes off to join me in the bathtub. As soon as he gets in, water splashes over the edge, creating a rather large puddle.

"Oops," he says with a sheepish grin. "Let me put down some extra towels." He gets back out and grabs two extra towels from under the sink and lays them out on the floor next to the tub to soak up the water. He gets back in and I shriek out in laughter at the huge tidal wave of water that escapes from the tub when he sits down. I open my legs to accommodate him as he situates himself on top of me.

"Hmm, how I've missed you today," he murmurs as his lips meet mine in a heart searing kiss. I moan and kiss him back just as ardently as he is kissing me. We continue like this for minutes before he starts making his way down my neck to my breasts to claim one of my nipples. I arch my back as he uses his tongue to tease and torture my sensitive bud. Wanting to give him as much pleasure as he's giving me, I rub my hands down his hard abs until I find his hard erection against his belly. I take it in my hand and start squeezing it, rubbing it up and down, imagining how good it is going to feel inside of me.

"Did you miss me, baby? Did you miss the feeling of me inside of you?" His husky voice taunts as he moves from one breast to the other to give both of them equal attention.

"Yes," I moan as his lips latch onto my other nipple, waves of desire drowning out my earlier fears. The need to have him inside me, to feel that connection that we have when we are together grows stronger, demanding that I satisfy my hunger for him.

"Switch positions with me," I demand when I can't take the yearning for him anymore. More water splashes over the edge of the tub as I slide out from underneath him to now be the one on top. I brace one hand against the tubs edge and guide myself down onto his hard cock. I hiss as he slowly fills me, stopping when I'm completely full of him. I slowly start rocking my hips back and forth, the motion making the tiny space of the tub turn into a wave pool. His mouth is wide open, his eyes hooded with passion as he watches our bodies be connected as one.

I increase my speed, rocking faster and faster, the buildup of my orgasm getting stronger and stronger. I grip the sides of the tub and tighten my thighs against his hips while I rub myself harder and faster against him. I watch his face start to contort into ecstasy as his orgasm hits, making mine explode inside of me. He grabs my hips, grinding the last of his release in me. I breathlessly fall against him, wrapping my arms around his neck and place my head against his chest.

I listen to his heartbeat's pulse slowly come back down to normal and pray that it never beats like that for anyone else ever again.

Twenty-One

Sean

Anticipation is buzzing through my veins, making my heart pump exceedingly fast with adrenaline. It isn't because we are in the limo, heading to Leicester Square for the world premiere of our new blockbuster movie. No, that's no big deal in my world. My anticipation is racing on revealing to the whole world who my girlfriend is.

And then finding a bathroom so I can have my way with her.

Isla rendered me speechless with her beauty when I met her in Cal and Jenna's suite at our hotel. Kellan got both women ready together, working his magic in outfitting them in luxurious dresses that mold their bodies to perfection. Not that he needed much magic, since both women are exquisite without all the makeup and hair extensions.

Isla is wearing a black lace, form fitting, floor length dress with a low neck line and thigh high slit to show off her shapely legs. I approve of this trend and hope it stays in fashion for a very long time since it gives me easier access to some of my favorite parts on her. She keeps looking down at her breasts and patting her fingers on the fabric, making sure her double sided tape is still there. I can't help but smile at how cute her nervousness is. If there weren't so many people in the car with us, I would check the tape myself for her.

The car pulls up to the curb of our destination, the red carpet and bright lights drawing our attention. One of the event staff comes to the window to see our credentials before checking us in and instructing us on the order of the procession line. Cal quickly kisses Jenna before they make their way out first. Isla and I watch while they walk hand in hand down the line to the first marker for photos. They take a couple shots together and then Jenna moves to the side for Cal's solo shots. My gaze moves past them and notices a tall woman, wearing a red dress almost identical to the red carpet on the floor, getting her photo taken. I take a closer look and suck in my breath as I recognize the woman as none other than Cora. I almost have to do a double take because I barely recognize her. While the color of her dress is attention grabbing, it is modest in style compared to Cora's previous red-carpet appearances. She's wearing a halter top dress that crosses around her neck, with the remaining part of the dress reaching the floor. Her hair is down in waves, as opposed to her usually off the face style. I wait to see if my body reacts and smile in happiness when nothing happens. In the past, my dick would have been standing to attention at the sight of her, my heart racing with hope that tonight would be the night that she finally sees me, and not just through me. But none of those old feelings come up to the surface, confirming what I was finally feeling.

That I'm in love with Isla.

I fell hard and fast for her, not really wanting to believe that this is what love felt like. It feels so easy and natural, that at first, I was in denial that it was actually what I was feeling.

But it *is* what I'm feeling and I was a damn fool for wasting all this time on someone who never felt the same way for me.

I need to tell Isla, since I know she has been feeling insecure with our relationship, especially with coming back into contact with Cora again. But now is not the appropriate time to say it, because I want to make it as special for her as it is to me.

"Is that Cora?" Isla whispers to me, her mouth dropped in

awe because even she can recognize how beautiful Cora is. I nod my head yes and see her gulp. Wanting to put her at ease, I squeeze her hand, turn her chin toward me so that she's forced to look into my eyes, and give her a soft peck on the lips.

"As far as I'm concerned, you are the most beautiful girl at the premiere tonight." That rewards me with a smile and another quick chaste kiss, which she wipes right off my lips in order to remove any remnants of lipstick.

The door to the limo is pulled open, indicating it is now our turn. I smooth out my suit jacket and get ready to exit out of the limo.

"Ready?" I ask her and squeeze her hand in encouragement. Her eyes are as wide as saucers, looking like she's a deer caught in headlights. She shakes her head no, takes a deep breath, and closes her eyes. She gives herself a thirty-second mental pep talk, and when she opens her eyes back up, confidence radiates out of them.

"I'm ready to show the world that Sean Lindsey is officially *off* the market now." I throw my head back in laughter, not expecting that answer, but loving it nonetheless. We get out of the car, ready to conquer this premiere together.

"Is it just me, or does Cora look like she's high as a kite?" Robert asks, watching Cora from a distance. Robert and I are standing at one of the high-top bar tables, enjoying a cocktail before I have to start mingling again. Cal and I don't usually watch the actual movie at the premieres, so we escorted our ladies straight to the after party, where a lot of the studio executives were waiting. Once the movie ended, the media and other invited guests made their way in for us to talk with.

I look over at Cora and do notice that her eyelids look droopy, a goofy smile resting permanently on her lips. She is sitting in a booth with Philip, listening to whatever he is saying to her, nodding her head at him. They share a laugh and then clink their glasses together. As if sensing that she is being watched, she meets my gaze, smiles warmly at me, and blows me a kiss. I salute her with my drink and turn my attention back to Robert.

"She's definitely in a good mood. Maybe she has found the old Cora, because this is the woman who used to be our best friend." Cora has been happy and calm all night long, a far cry from the Cora who we have seen the last couple of years. She was even cordial to Jenna and Isla when we all met up on the red carpet for photos. Sure, that could have all been for the camera's sake, but her demeanor has not shown a glimpse of the vicious Cora…yet. I really want to give her the benefit of the doubt, because I'm rooting for a healthy Cora who finds love with someone.

"Why is it taking Isla so long to go to the restroom?" I send her another text, asking her where she is, but get no response. It has been at least ten minutes and while I know the party is crowded, it shouldn't take her that long. I search out the crowd and finally get a glimpse of her profile. She is talking to some good-looking guy and immediately my blood starts to boil with jealousy.

"Who is that guy Isla is talking to?" Robert usually knows everyone in the industry since becoming one of Cal's assistant as well, so I'm hoping he'll know who I have to give fair warning to stay away from my girlfriend.

"You are like a dog in heat or something, calm it down. He's some no name actor who she went to boarding school with. And he's gay, so don't get your undies all wadded up." I watch as he whispers something into her ear that makes her laugh. He motions his finger to another room and starts walking in that direction, with Isla following him. Not wanting anyone else taking more of her time away from me, I excuse myself from Robert and decide to go follow them.

I get into the next room, only to find it empty. I see another door that looks like it leads outside and I'm about to reach it when I hear my name called from behind.

"Sean!" Cora runs in, breathing heavily from trying to catch up with me. "There you are! I wanted to have a quick word with you alone since we haven't had time to officially catch up."

"Now is really not the best time. I'm trying to find Isla, but we can catch up tomorrow when we leave for Paris," I suggest, really wanting to get Isla and leave. The idea of not seeing her for the next three days makes me eager to get her back to the hotel and worship her body as much as I physically can tonight.

"Absolutely!" Cora agrees a little too enthusiastically. As I inspect her more closely, I'm now convinced that she is high on something. Her pupils are dilated, her speech is slow, and she isn't taking the hint that I can't talk right now. "I just want to thank you again for caring about me enough to keep in touch while I was in treatment. Your texts helped me get through some really dark days, so I just wanted to personally thank you." Before I realize what she's doing, she throws her arms around my neck and starts kissing me.

And I don't mean the friend like peck.

She starts trying to full-blown make out with me.

I grab her arms from around my neck and push her away when I hear a loud gasp of shock from behind me. I turn around to see Isla standing in the doorway, hand over her heart, pain blazing from her eyes. Before I can even blink, she turns around and runs into the sea of people in the crowd.

"Isla!" I shout and run after her, trying to keep my focus on her head as I push and shove people out of my way. By the time I weave my way through everyone to get to the entrance, she is long gone.

"*Fuck!*" I scream out at no one, wrapping my hand around the back of my neck and looking up toward the sky. *How could this be happening to me?* I grab my phone out of my pocket to call her. Her phone goes straight to voicemail. I leave a message, insisting that the kiss was not what it seemed, begging her to call me.

"Sean!" I hear my name and cringe at the sight of Cora coming toward me. "Sean, I'm so sorry! I don't know what came over me. I missed you so much and was hoping that you missed me as well. I thought maybe we could try to start to be more than friends. I didn't realize that you and Isla were in a committed relationship." When I refuse to answer her, she reaches out to touch my arm. "Sean, I'm sorry, I—"

"*Don't fucking touch me!*" I yell, causing her to flinch and snatch her hand back. "Everything you touch, you destroy." And with that, I run out to the street to get a taxi and go back to the hotel. I keep calling Isla the whole ride back. She still refuses to answer.

I decide to take the stairs up to our room, not taking any chances of the elevator getting stuck or having too many people on it. When I arrive, the room is empty, everything exactly as we left it. While pacing through the room, wondering how I'm going to find Isla, my phone vibrates with a message.

Isla: I'm staying at an old friend's house from boarding school. I need you to leave me alone. You made me fall in love with you, only to shatter my heart into a million pieces. You can go fuck yourself! Enjoy your miserable life with Cora.

I re-read her text message two more times before hurling my phone against the wall, not caring if it made a dent.

Living without Isla is not even an option.

I have to win her back.

Twenty-Two

Sean

THE PLANE RIDE to Paris is pretty torturous for me, considering my heart is being left behind in London. I barely slept, hoping that if I was up early enough, Isla would come back to get her belongings and we could talk. Instead, she had Jenna retrieve them and was going straight to the Harrington's London home from her friend's house that she slept at. She continues to ignore my calls and texts. My only ray of hope right now is Jenna. Brooks was sick last night, so Jenna is not accompanying us to Paris. When I explained to her what happened, she didn't hesitate in believing me. I know Jenna senses that I have fallen for Isla. She has never seen me act this before—even with Cora—so she promised she would try to talk with Isla for me.

I'm pulled out of my thoughts when one of the movie studio publicists sits down next to me to go over the itinerary for Paris and Berlin. The studio chartered this plane for the press tour and everyone who needs to be here is on it—directors, producers, main actors, assistants, publicists, and agents. It is stifling, loud, and with my current mood, annoying. I just want to be left the hell alone to think. Cal and Robert understand as they are sitting somewhere else on the plane, away from me. Fortunately, with being in the industry as long as I have, my meeting with the publicist is short since she is confident that I know what I'm doing. Once she leaves me alone, I go back to brooding while looking out of the window, hoping no one else will bother me for the remainder of the flight.

My thoughts wander back to Isla and how we're going to get past the first bump in our relationship. I'm angry that she has given up so easily on us. I'm also disappointed that she didn't believe me when I said I wasn't a willing participant in that kiss. I know with my past feelings for Cora and the newness of our relationship, there was still doubt in her mind and unfortunately, I did nothing to squash that doubt. Isla didn't like the frequency of the texting that was going on between Cora and me, but I made it clear to her that Cora has been one of my best friends, and that I wasn't giving up on that part of our relationship. I wasn't going to abandon her like everyone else has in her life.

Maybe that was the wrong decision.

Maybe I should've reassured Isla of my feelings for her.

Maybe I should've told her I was falling in love with her.

I would be an asshole if I sat here and didn't try to think of Isla's point of view. If the roles were reversed and I walked in on what she did, I probably would've done the same thing—except, I would've beaten the shit out of whomever was kissing her and *then* I would've told her it was over. I probably wouldn't be returning her calls or texts either until I had a chance to calm down and think things through. With that in mind, I agree that Isla deserves time to cool down, but I'm not going to stop calling and texting her. She can send me to voicemail every time if she wants—I will fill that shit up until it's no longer accepting messages.

I text my assistant, telling her I need two bouquets of flowers delivered to Isla every single day while I'm away. Then I send another text to Isla for the fourth time this morning.

Me: You're the best thing that has ever happened to me. I'm not giving up on us.

"Sean, can we talk for a minute?" Cora asks, interrupting my text.

Cora is the last person I want to talk to, but she's right in that we do need to talk about what happened last night. She needs to know that our relationship will always be *just* friends. She also needs to understand how important Isla is to me.

I hit send on my text to Isla and jerk my head toward the seat facing me for her to sit down. She cautiously sits on the edge of it, her hands folded neatly in her lap with her legs pressed together. She's wearing another modest outfit today of a black, button-down long sleeve silk top with taupe colored dress slacks and black high heels. Her hair is pulled back into a ponytail and her makeup is light and natural. She's portraying the look of classic elegance, two words that I never thought would be put together in the same sentence to describe her.

"I want to apologize for my behavior last night. As I said, I hadn't realized you were in a serious relationship considering you weren't the last time I saw you."

"Things can happen quickly in one month. I fell in love and now I'm in a committed relationship, one that I demand you have respect for." My stare never waivers from hers, hoping she can read that I'm dead serious from my body language and tone.

"Love?" Her eyes are wide with surprise at my admission. "How can you be in love with her when you have been in love with me all these years?"

"Easy, since it was quite apparent that I've been in love with the wrong person all this time. Isla gives me her love unconditionally and freely, with no strings attached and no expectations. Something you were never willing to ever give me."

"Sean, darling, don't you think that maybe you're confusing love with lust? I know you were going through a rather dry spell from sex while hanging out at Cal's house for a while." She winks at me, the action making my blood boil at her demeaning attitude toward my new relationship.

"I'm one hundred percent accurate in my feelings for Isla since they're much more intense than any feelings I've ever had for you." I stare at her coldly, ready for her to leave me the hell alone. I deliver the punch and see the affect it has on her. She winces and then swallows whatever she was about to say next.

"That was really hurtful, Sean. I'm just trying to be a good friend. I know you're angry with me, so I'll let your words slide since you aren't being yourself. All I care about is your happiness, so if you're happy, I'm happy." She gets up to stand, leaving me speechless as to who this person in front of me is supposed to be.

"I'm truly happy for you, Sean. Maybe after you've had a chance to calm down, you can tell me all about her and what the future holds for you." I watch her walk away and sit down in a seat closer to the front of the plane.

As the captain announces our descent into Paris and asks us to return to our seats, I can't help but wonder if he has just flown us into the *Twilight Zone*.

Twenty-Three

Cora

I KEEP MY smile plastered on my face while I walk the hotel hallway to my room, nodding at people who greet me as I walk by them. Once inside my room and the door closed behind me, I breathe a sigh of relief to have a few moments to myself and not have to act anymore.

As soon as we got off the plane, Cal, Sean, and I went straight to the press junket to promote our movie. Sitting there for hours on end with journalists who ask you the same questions over and over again—some so stupid and have no relevance to the movie—is emotionally draining. Being a nice person to people is fucking exhausting! All the chitty chatter, the smiling, the laughing, the pretending to care about others who don't give a rat's ass about you … *ugh*!

I look at my watch to see I only have a couple of hours before I have to start getting ready for the premiere tonight. With last night in London being considered the world premiere of the movie, our time in Paris is very limited. Similar to yesterday's schedule, we premiere the movie, go to the after party, and then leave for Berlin the following morning. Due to some scheduling conflicts in Berlin, our press junket there is planned out for most of the day, with the premiere being the following day. We get two days in Berlin, whereas here, we only get one. After Berlin, we get almost two weeks off before our press junkets and premieres in the United States. With Cal and Sean going back to London for their time off when we're done in Berlin, my window of opportunity of getting Cal alone is decreasing by the second. That makes today the day to execute my plan.

The plan came to me in my last week of treatment. I was having horrible anxiety and insomnia, panicking over how I was going to win Cal when all the cards were stacked against me. The lack of sleep was starting to become evident during my therapy sessions, so they prescribed me Rohypnol to try. Because it's such a powerfully addictive drug, the nurses were in charge of administering my doses. Every night I had to check in at the facility run pharmacy, where they would give me one pill before bed time and make me take it in front of them. The first night of taking it was the best night of sleep I've ever had in my life. I woke up the next morning feeling like I was hungover, but as the day wore on, I actually felt well rested. With my body starting to get used to it on a consistent basis, the hungover feeling started to fade, while the well-rested feeling only increased. I stopped feeling tired and my anxiety was almost non-existent. I was in love with my new magic happy pill and decided to do some research on how I can get more and why it was so powerful that some countries ban it. I was actually quite appalled when reading the stories of despicable people using it to drug others to have sex with them. *Why would you even want to have sex with someone who was unresponsive?*

And then the light bulb went off in my head.

I can lure Cal to my room by himself, a crushed-up Rohypnol waiting for him to drink in a cocktail that I provide. Because it will make him lucid within fifteen minutes, I should have no problems putting ourselves in compromising positions that Danny can take photos of. Then he can sell the story and be published all over the world, making Cal look like a cheating bastard.

The treatment facility just went from being hell to heaven

with supplying me the key to my plan.

Goodbye, Jenna!

Because of how dangerous Rohypnol can be, I can only buy a tiny supply off the black market from southeast Asia. Fortunately, I received my package the day before the London premiere. In my giddiness to having it back, I decided to crush one up and snort it like I do with my cocaine before the premiere in order to calm my nerves.

Big mistake.

I was barely functioning at one point during the night from the high of the drug. Fortunately, I kept pumping water in me, making multiple trips to the bathroom to try to pee it out of my system. I was surprised at how quickly the high hits you when you're snorting it, compared to swallowing the pill as a whole. I think that from now on, I will stick to my good friend cocaine to snort before any public events.

My phone buzzes with a message from Danny, alerting me of his arrival in Paris. I send him a response back with my hotel information, telling him he needs to pick up a bottle of high-end whiskey for Cal's drink. Once he has confirmed, I start getting myself ready for the big event. I go to my suitcase to retrieve the lingerie I bought for this specific occasion. I take out a black lace baby doll negligee and slip it on. I then cover myself up with a matching robe that stops at mid-thigh. I keep my makeup on since it was already done for the press junket, but I run a flat iron through my hair to freshen it up. Next, I get my bottle of Rohypnol out of its hiding place in my toiletries case and start smashing one up. Since Cal is a much larger person than I, two might be the best for him. I add the second pill and smash it up with the bottom of a glass. Once the pills are in powder form, I pour it into the glass, ready for the whiskey to be added to it.

Danny arrives ten minutes later with the whiskey and his camera. "So what's the plan?" He questions, his eyes narrow as his gaze travels up and down my body. Suddenly, I'm creeped out and conscious of the fact that I'm alone with him in a hotel room.

"The plan is for you to hide in the closet when Cal arrives and as soon as you see us kissing, start taking pictures."

"How are you going to get him to kiss you? The man looks at you as if he doesn't even like you, let alone him being madly in love with his wife."

"Don't worry about how I get him to comply. Just worry about getting the shot." I smile smugly at him, wanting him to focus on getting the job done right.

"You're right, the less I know, the better. How are you going to get him to come to your room?"

"I'm going to text him, saying I'm concerned with the lack of jobs our agent has not been getting me and if he can come here and talk to me about how I should handle the situation. I'm banking on Cal's kindness to want to help me. He will especially want to hear how Philip is not doing his job."

"Hmm, I don't buy it. I don't think he's going to fall for that," he says with so much conviction, that doubt starts to creep in about if my plan will actually work. I shake my head to get the negative thoughts out since I don't have time for this. It *has* to work!

"Well, let's see who's right by getting this show on the road." I walk over to the table and pour the whiskey in its designated glass. I send Cal the text and wait with anticipation. He doesn't disappoint and responds right away.

Cal: Sure, I'll be there in twenty minutes.

I show Danny the text with a satisfied, smug grin on my face, loving the fact that I know Cal better than anyone.

"This calls for a celebration!" I walk over to the mini bar and pour myself a glass of champagne. I then quickly put a line of cocaine together. I snort every last drop into my nose, throw my head back, and then wipe off any remnants. "Want some?" I offer my rolled-up straw to Danny, but he declines. I tidy up my mess and put away the evidence. Danny starts getting his camera gear ready and puts the bag in my closet where he will be stationed.

"How long do you think this is going to take?" He asks, putting his camera strap around his neck, ready for action.

"Why, have a hot date tonight? I'm paying you a lot of money to be at my beck and call here. It'll take however long we need it to take in order to get the perfect shot," I snap and before I can tear into him some more, a knock is at my door.

"It hasn't been twenty minutes yet, has it?" I whisper, wondering how much time has passed since our text message exchange. I tiptoe over to the door and look through the peephole to see Sean standing on the other side.

"Oh shit, hide in my bathroom!" I softly hiss, trying to figure out what to say to get Sean to leave quickly.

"Cora, I know you're in there. Can I talk to you for a second?" Sean knocks at the door again, his voice muffled by the door.

"Just a minute!" I shout as I watch Danny scurry into the bathroom and shut the door behind him. I tighten the sash around my robe, push my hair off my face, and take a deep breath before opening the door.

"Sean, what a nice surprise! What can I do for you?" I stand in my doorway, trying to avoid inviting him in.

"These are for you." He brings out a bouquet of flowers from around his back, the gesture making me genuinely surprised. "I was pretty harsh to you on the plane and it was uncalled for, so I wanted to apologize."

I grab the bouquet and bring it to my face, taking a deep breath to look like I'm enjoying them, when in reality, I hate flowers. They are the stupidest gift ever since they eventually die and you have nothing to keep in the end. "That's so incredibly sweet of you, Sean. You truly didn't have to. Like I said on the plane, I knew that wasn't the real you talking and I forgave you."

"Well, thank you for that. Listen, can I come in? I would really like to talk more with you about Isla and my concerns on how we're going to maintain a friendship if you two aren't getting along."

I swallow and smile brightly, having no excuse to tell him no. I move to the side so he can walk past me into the suite. I close the door behind him and pray that Cal isn't on time for once in his life.

"Let me just go put these in water real quick. I'll be right back." I grab the ice bucket and take the bouquet into the bathroom, shutting the door as soon as I enter. Danny is standing right by the door, his eyes wide with panic. I hold up my finger to my lips for him to be silent when he tries to whisper something to me. I turn on the faucet and motion for him to go back in the corner. Once the bucket is full, I take it back outside and stop short at the sight of Sean pouring whiskey into another glass.

Fuck, which glass is the right one for Cal?

He smiles and comes toward me with both glasses. "I saw that you got one of my favorite whiskeys and were going to have a drink without me, so I poured another glass. We can each have one and toast to new beginnings." He hands me a glass and I stare at it in uncertainty, not being able to tell which glass has the Rohypnol in it.

"So here's to new beginnings as friends! "He clinks our glasses together and I can only stand there and watch in horror as he downs the whole drink.

"Well, don't just stand there and stare at your drink. Down it!" He sees me hesitate and looks at me in suspicion. "Don't tell me you don't like whiskey anymore? We were doing shots of that on the last day of our movie together."

I look down into my glass and pray to God that my drink is the spiked one. I give him a weak smile and down the whiskey. It burns going down my esophagus and for once, I welcome the pain that I deserve and so much more for what I'm about to put Sean through if his was the wrong drink.

He grabs my glass from my hand and heads back over to the table where he pours two more glasses of whiskey. I have to somehow distract him from drinking anymore or he's going to be in grave danger if his had the Rohypnol in it.

"Sean, why don't we sit down and you start talking about what you wanted to discuss?" I sit down on the couch, hoping he doesn't bring his glass with him, but of course, he not only brings his glass, but mine as well. He puts the glasses down on the coffee table and sits down next to me, twisting his body so that he's facing me.

"We've been friends for a long time, Cora, and I really would hate for that friendship to end just because you and Isla don't like each other. Do you know what reasons she may have for not liking you?"

I grit my teeth, not caring why that little slut doesn't like me. If Sean did drink the Rohypnol, she'll have even more reason to hate me. Fear is setting in as the implications of what could be happening start to dance around in my head. I've got to get Sean back to his room so Danny can get the hell out of here before things get really bad. One of us is going to be down for the count soon and an ambulance will be called. Danny's presence in my bathroom will be a tough one to lie my way out of. As soon as Cal and Sean see him, they will know that I have been conspiring with the man who is their enemy.

"I don't know why she hates me, Sean. Maybe all three of us should sit down together and figure it out?"

"That's actually a really good idea. Maybe when we get back home, we can schedule a time together." I watch him carefully, so far seeing no side effects from him and so far, I'm still feeling fine. I hear a knock on the door and my heart races with acknowledgement that it's probably Cal, and that my moment with him alone is now completely ruined.

"You expecting someone?" Sean raises one of his eyebrow in question.

I give him a smile in defeat, knowing that all hell is going to break loose any moment now. "It's Cal. I wanted to talk with him about my unhappiness with Philip."

"Oh really? I didn't know you were unhappy with him." Sean stands up, taking another sip of whiskey as he does.

I slowly make my way to the door, not wanting to answer it, because as soon as I do, my living nightmare will begin.

Cal is in the same clothes he was in during the press junket, looking devastatingly handsome in a charcoal button-down shirt and black slacks. I take a moment to memorize his face, the sharp edges of his cheekbones, the cleft in his chin, his strong nose and lastly, those blue eyes. Those eyes that I wanted to stare into forever.

Goodbye, my love.

He greets me with a nod, walks in, and is surprised to see Sean. "Oh good, I didn't realize Cora invited you here too. We can all talk this over together about Philip and what problems you are having."

Just as I'm about to close the door behind Cal, I notice Sean starting to blink rapidly.

No.

He starts to sway where he stands, his hand going over his heart.

Oh my god, no!

His eyelids start to droop and he stumbles.

"Sean, are you okay?" Cal watches in concern as he slowly makes his way toward him.

I'm so sorry, Sean!

Sean shakes his head back and forth and takes one last look at me.

"What did you do to me?" he whispers before his legs give out.

"*No!*" I scream as I watch in slow motion Sean falling to the floor, his head bouncing off the corner of the coffee table. Cal runs forward, yelling to dial for an ambulance.

Tears start streaming down my face as I place the call for help, running into the bathroom to get towels to stop the blood that is coming out of Sean's head. Danny springs out of the bathroom and races straight for the door. Cal watches him in stunned silence and then looks at me, understanding starting to set in his eyes.

I just played Russian Roulette with my life … and lost everything.

Twenty-Four

Isla

I WAS INCONSOLABLE during the hour-long flight to Paris, so much so, that I threw up three times at the thought that Sean might be dead. Jenna tried her best to comfort me, repeating over and over again that he's going to be fine, but I refuse to believe it until I see him for myself.

"What if he's not, Jenna? That stuff is so dangerous by itself, but mixed with alcohol?" I start to cry again. "Why would she do this?"

"We just have to keep praying that he's going to be okay, Isla," Jenna soothes as she continues to rub my back, her eyes red from crying as well.

Robert has a car waiting for us when we disembark from the plane. He has been texting Jenna non-stop, giving her the play-by-play of what is happening at the hospital. It has now been close to four hours since Sean ingested the Rohypnol and he's still unconscious. The longer he stays that way, the likelihood that he might stay in a coma.

I *refuse* to even think about that.

Forty minutes later, we pull up to the hospital, a grave looking Robert waiting outside for us.

"Is he awake?" I question the second I'm out of the car.

Robert gives me a sad smile and shakes his head no. He

motions for us to follow him and walks us through the hospital to the elevators. "I must warn you both, Cora is still here with a police escort. She's requesting to see Sean, but Cal won't let anyone in the room until you arrive. He has a guard standing outside Sean's door. Danny Salari has been released already from custody and is at the airport to go back home. Since he wasn't the one who provided the drugs to Cora, they couldn't charge him. He claims he had no idea what her plans were. Just that he was told to hide in the closet and take photos of her in compromising positions. He was told by Cora that it was going to be with Cal."

I gasp in shock and look at Jenna. She's staring at Robert, at first in disbelief, but then her face changes to stone, her eyes giving away the rage that is brewing, like molten lava ready to erupt from the peak of a volcano. The dinging noise of the elevator's arrival to our destination brings her out of her trance.

Once the doors open, the first person we see is Cora. She's flanked by two police officers on each side. Her wrists are in handcuffs in front of her, her mascara caked down her cheeks from crying, her eyes wild with fright. She's wearing her silk robe that is open, exposing a sexy negligee underneath. I ball my hands into fists at the sight of her, refusing to look at her as we walk out of the elevators.

"Jenna … Jenna, wait! I need to see Sean! Please convince Cal that I need to see him." She's out of her chair faster than the policemen can stop her and runs to stand in front of Jenna, blocking her path. She grabs Jenna's arm with her cuffed hands, begging her to listen.

"Get out of my way," Jenna warns, her voice cold, menace in her eyes. She refuses to look at Cora and focuses past her to the guard that is stationed outside of what we presume is Sean's room.

"Jenna, please! I love Sean and—" Before Cora can finish her sentence, Jenna yanks her arm out from Cora's grasp and in lightning speed, slaps Cora across the face. The force of the slap snaps Cora's head to the side, causing her to lose her balance and fall. The two policemen pick her up and haul her back up to her feet. She stumbles and looks at Jenna in shock, blood trickling down the corner of her mouth.

"You've never loved Sean! You've never loved anyone but yourself! He has always been a pawn in your sick, delusional game. You deserve an eternity in hell!" Jenna screams while Robert and I block her from attacking Cora any further. Philip and Cal must have heard the commotion inside of Sean's room, as they come racing down the hallway toward us.

"What's going on here?" Philip asks, looking between all of us for answers. Cal doesn't say a word, just walks straight to Jenna and takes her in his arms.

"She attacked me for no reason! I'm going to sue you for everything you're worth!" Cora shrieks while she tries to charge Jenna, but the policemen prevent her from doing so.

"You have no case since it was self-defense. I have witnesses here who saw you touch me first, you stupid bitch," Jenna responds, her voice calm while she stays engulfed in Cal's arms. If I wasn't so distraught over Sean right now, I would hug Jenna for doing what we all have wanted to do for a long time.

"Philip, it's time for you to escort her to Qatar for her previously scheduled appearance," Cal orders and then looks at Cora, his eyes completely void of all emotion. "Restraining orders have been placed against you. If you ever come as close to an inch to me, Sean, and our respective families, I will have you hauled off to a psychiatric ward, where you will be locked up in forever."

"Cal, *please*," she whispers as she cries, looking completely broken and defeated.

"Consider not being arrested and sent to a Parisian prison for you to rot in a parting gift." He unwraps his arms from Jenna, grabs her hand, and motions for Robert and me to start following him. "We're done here, Philip. Please get her out of my sight." The wails of Cora's cries fill the air while we walk away from her to Sean's room. All of us sigh in relief when the elevator doors close, indicating she's gone.

I truly pray that she's gone from our lives forever.

We approach Sean's door and Cal introduces us to the guard so he knows we're allowed into Sean's room at any given time. I reach for the door handle, but Cal touches my arm to stop me. "Isla, I just want to warn you that he doesn't look good. He hit his head when he lost consciousness and when the medics arrived, his face was turning blue from lack of oxygen. They don't know how it has affected him yet. You might want to try to talk to him as much as you can. It's imperative that he wakes up, Isla." Cal's voice cracks, tears forming in his eyes. Jenna wraps her arms around his waist, squeezing him for comfort. Cal swallows and smiles at her to show he's okay. "Let's give Isla some privacy with him. We'll be right out here if you need us." He squeezes my hand and takes Jenna to where Robert and Kellan are seated.

I close my eyes and pray that Sean doesn't look as bad as I'm picturing him to look. I grab the handle, slowly turn it, and push the door open as softly as I can. I close the door behind me and walk to the bed to be closer to him. When my eyes focus on his face, I cry out in horror at the sight of him.

He looks worse than I could've imagined.

His head is wrapped in a bandage, dried up blood from where he hit his head showing through the gauze. From what I can see of his face that's not covered by the oxygen mask, his color looks ashen. Sean is a strong, muscular man, but lying here in bed, he looks frail and delicate. I pull a chair to his bedside and grab his hand, kissing every inch of his palm and fingers, my tears starting to make small puddles on his skin. I smear the wetness across his skin, praying that maybe the shock of the moisture might wake him up.

"Sean, honey, you owe me a trip to Paris, because this was not how I was picturing my first time back here would be like." I try to make a joke, but it's hard when the situation is anything but funny. I keep rubbing my thumb across the back of his hand, trying to think of what to say when all I want to do is curl up in his hospital bed and hold him.

"I need you to wake up, Sean. I need you to yell at me for running away again, or more preferably, kiss me and tell me you forgive me." I study his face, watching his eye lashes closely to see if I can see any movement, but there's none.

"This can't be the end of our narrative, Sean. I refuse for it to end this way. We have only just begun and our story is pretty epic, if I do say so myself." I hate how the only sound I hear is the beeping of his heart monitor, so I decide to keep talking, even if none of it makes any sense.

"I think you have always known I had a crush on you when we were growing up, but do you know when I actually realized I loved you? It was when our families were on vacation in Santorini when we were kids. You walked in on me putting on my bathing suit." I start to giggle at the memory of how horrified I was that he just barged right into my room without even knocking, something that he still does to this day. "You just continued staring at me while I was trying to cover myself up. Finally, you looked at me and said those were the smallest mosquito bites you had ever seen in your life and turned around and left! I already had a complex about how everyone in my class had tits but me, so I couldn't believe you said that to me." I shake my head at the memory since he really was a piece of shit that day for saying that. "The look on your face when I called you the ugliest wanker on the planet was priceless, but it was how you looked at me later on that evening, when you came to apologize, is what did me in. Those gorgeous eyes of yours had remorse and sympathy. When you told me you were sorry and then hugged me as I struggled not to cry … I knew it was your arms I wanted to be in forever."

I need him to wake up and laugh with me at this memory, and all the memories I have of us from childhood. Anger starts to rise up, making me livid that he hasn't woken yet. He is strong and young, he should be awake by now.

"Wake up, Sean! Wake the fuck *up!* How dare you come back into my life after I thought I finally got over you and make me fall in love with you again! How dare you try to leave me this way! Do you know that you are making Cal cry? Cal! The man with the scary, hot, intense face. He's out there crying for you. We all need you to wake up! Avery is going to be so angry with you if her Uncle Sean doesn't wake up. *Wake up!*" I finally scream, not caring if everyone outside these walls hears me yelling at him. "I will not accept this from you! You are a fighter and have so much to live for. Stop hiding in there and wake up!" I yell more, tears running down my cheeks. I start pushing at him, hoping for some sort of reflex, hoping that the movement will jolt him awake.

I'm hoping for a miracle.

When I keep pushing and pushing at him and nothing happens, my hope turns into despair and I throw myself down on the bed, clutching his arm, my sobs shaking my body to my core. I grip his hand in mine, my cheek resting on top of it, and close my eyes, savoring the memories that are on replay in my mind.

Visions of us as children together.

Visions of us as adults, seeing each other for the very first time in Vancouver after all those years. I still can feel the jolt of electricity when his eyes met mine, recognizing who he was seeing and liking what he saw.

Visions of him kissing me for the first time, the way his face looked as his lips slowly descended upon mine.

Visions of him when he was deep inside of me, the look of ecstasy on his face when he came.

I don't feel my tears being brushed away from cheek at first, too numb from my pain to feel anything than what the memories are making me feel right now.

But then I notice it.

I feel the tiniest flicker of his finger.

I bolt up and stare at his hand. His finger, at a snail's pace, is waving at me. I gasp as my eyes slowly travel to his chest, seeing it rise up and down, faster than it was before. My gaze continues up to his face and for a moment, nothing happens, making me wonder if I'm now delusional with my grief.

But then his eyelids move, and I see a tiny sliver of those beautiful green eyes.

"*Nurse!*" I start screaming and run from my chair to open the door. "He's awake!" I yell out to the hallway and run back into the room and grab his hand, not waiting to see if anyone else is coming.

"Sean, Sean … can you hear me? Blink if you can hear me!" He slowly blinks and I exhale out in relief, thanking God numerous times that my love is going to be okay. I place my forehead on his chest and cry happy tears of joy that this is not going to be his ending—or ours. I move out of the way when the nurse comes rushing in and start quickly checking his vitals. Cal, Jenna, Robert and Kellan come in after, congregating at the foot of the bed, hope shining brightly from their tear-soaked eyes.

"I'm going to go get the doctor to check him out," the nurse tells us and leaves the room.

Sean turns over his hand, his palm facing up for me to place my hand in. I grab his hand and bring it up to my lips, showering it with kisses of love. He starts to take off his oxygen mask in order for him to talk.

"Sean, don't do that just yet," I chide as I stand up to put the mask back on. He shakes his head at me and motions for me to come closer so he can whisper in my ear. I lean in close so he doesn't have to strain his voice.

"I want your mosquito bites to be mine forever," he teases, his voice hoarse from not being in use. I burst out laughing, fresh tears coming down my face as I softly kiss his lips. A lone tear slides out of his right eye and I wipe it away with my thumb, caressing his cheek with love.

"I love you, Isla. You're never allowed to leave me again," he rasps out and I nod in acknowledgement. No words are needed right now since he can see my love and adoration for him shining through my eyes.

The doctor comes in and I move out of the way, taking that opportunity to hug each of our friends. We look back over at Sean as the doctor examines him, telling him what his road to recovery will look like. We all can't contain our smiles of gratitude that Sean is going to be okay.

I SIT BACK in the lounge chair and prop my hands behind my head, sighing in contentment as I inhale the salt in the air from the ocean and admire the view that is before me. Most people sit on the beaches of St. Lucia and are mesmerized by the crystal-clear ocean of the Caribbean. I, on the other hand, am mesmerized by something else in the ocean.

Or should I say, someone in that ocean.

I'm mesmerized by the woman who taught me what true love feels like.

I'm mesmerized by the woman who is my fucking everything.

I'm mesmerized by the woman who I can't live a single day without.

After the incident with Cora, Isla and I went back to Ireland for two weeks where she nursed me back to health from the poisoning. We rejoined Cal and Jenna in the United States for the remainder of the press tour—a tour that Cora was no longer invited to be on. The studio sent out a press release saying she was unable to attend the premieres in New York and Los Angeles due to personal reasons.

One month later, it was all over the news that Cora had

married Prince Khalid Rashid al-Hamad in a private ceremony in the south of France. I have no doubt that she did it for the money, but maybe she also did it so she wouldn't feel so alone. Whatever her reasons may be, I only hope that she's finally at peace and happy. I have forgiven Cora for her wrong doings, but I will never forget how she almost destroyed my life.

"You look like you're drunk with that ridiculous smile on your face," Robert comments as he hands me a beer and sits down next to me. All of us have come to St. Lucia for Layla and Chase's wedding. The beautiful, emotional ceremony was held yesterday at sundown and today we're all recovering, enjoying our last day in paradise before we go back home.

"I am drunk … drunk on love, Robert." I chuckle as he rolls his eyes at me and looks out at my view. Kellan has joined Isla in the water and we watch the two of them laugh at something he says to her.

"You sure are and it looks damn good on you, Sean. I'm truly happy for the both of you." He leans over and gives my leg a hard slap. "So when are you going to make her an honest woman?"

"As soon as you marry Kellan." I raise my eyebrows in a challenge, wondering when those two are going to make it officially legal themselves.

"Ooh, a dual wedding! That sounds like fun, although Kellan might not like the attention taken away from him." He looks like he's seriously pondering the idea and I immediately regret my words.

"Rewind and forget what I just said to you. Her engagement ring is back home in my safe and I plan on proposing at the opening ceremony of her new school."

Isla quit her job as the nanny to the Harrington's six months ago. She moved in with me and focused on her dream of opening her own boarding school. With my help and some other celebrity investors that I put her in contact with, the construction of the school will be breaking ground shortly.

"You're going to wait two years to propose?" He looks at

me in disbelief and then shakes his head when I give him a questioning look, confused as to what he's talking about. "Did you not pay any attention at the architects meeting when they said it will be a two-year project?" I shake my head as I recollect that my attention was focused solely on my girlfriend and how hot she looked talking to the architects about the functionality of the school. My mind completely wondered from the topic of conversation to daydreaming of bending her over that desk and taking her from behind.

"Hell no, I'm not waiting two years to get engaged!" I growl and contemplate what it would take to maybe get engaged next weekend.

"Did someone say they're getting engaged?" Jenna's voice drifts over as she and Layla walk toward us with drinks in their hands. Layla is sipping a Pina Colada while Jenna is drinking sparkling water because Cal, once again, has gotten her pregnant. I look behind them to see that Cal and Chase are still standing at the bar, probably talking about business since Cal's an investor in Chase's family business.

"I have no idea what you're talking about," I respond, an innocent look on my face as I try to play naive. Jenna is going to expect details of how I plan to propose to Isla and quite frankly, I want to keep that a surprise.

"Oh c'mon, Sean. Don't keep me in suspense! I can help you plan," she whines, an evil smile spreading on my face as karma is a bitch and I'm getting her back for not telling me about their surprise wedding.

"Sucks to be left in the dark, doesn't it?" I laugh when she throws an ice cube at me. My phone suddenly rings in the cupholder of my chair. I look to see it's an international number that I don't recognize. Since I'm waiting to hear from a director on a new movie role that I've been wanting, I decide to answer the call and walk away from the group to have some privacy.

"Hello?" I answer and when the line stays silent, I say it one more time, prepared to hang up when a voice cuts through, barely audible.

"Sean? *Sean!* It's me, Sean. Please don't hang up on me! I know you don't want to hear from me, but I really need your help." I stiffen at a voice that I never wanted to hear from again.

Cora.

"How the hell did you get my new phone number?" I growl, and I move a little bit farther so no one can hear me.

"Sean, *please!* You've got to listen to me because I only have a minute to talk. I need you, Sean! I need you to get me out of here. Khalid forces me to do some very bad things. Things that are going to scar me for life. I am living in hell, Sean! You've got to get me out of here!" She pleads and for once, I feel nothing for her. While I hope what she's saying is not true, her words have zero credibility. She's cried wolf one too many times. I will not risk losing Isla to help Cora ever again.

"You're an addict and a liar, Cora. You're not my problem anymore. In fact, you're dead to me. Don't ever call me again." My voice is dead calm before I hang up on her and immediately block the number that she just used to call me from. I send my assistant a quick text, warning her that I plan on changing my phone number once again as soon as I get back home. I shut off my phone for the remainder of the day, refusing to let her tarnish my mood.

I make my way back to my chair, noticing that Cal and Chase have finally joined us. As I sit back down, Kellan and Isla decide to come out of the ocean. I stare at her as I watch her emerge, looking like a wet goddess. As if she knows exactly what I'm thinking, she gives me a playful smile before plopping her wet body down onto mine. I kiss her soundly on the lips and whisper I love you while staring directly into her eyes. She cradles my face in between her hands, her eyes baring right into me. "Are you okay?" she asks, her eyes narrowing in concern.

Avery's scream of laughter catches my attention as her new nanny brings her and Brooks back to Jenna and Cal from making sandcastles. I can't stop my gaze from looking at each and every single person in this group, noting how happy everyone is, how much we all support each other in good times and in bad. But most importantly, how we love each other wholeheartedly and without judgment. These are my people, my family, my tribe.

I look back at Isla and smile into her searching eyes. "I'm the happiest I've ever been in my whole entire life."

And I am.

Because I'm home.

Also by Jessica Marin

The Let Me In Series

Heartbreak Warfare (Let Me In, Book 1)

Perfectly Lonely (Let Me In, Book 2)

Edge of Desire (Let Me In, Book 3)

Half of My Heart (Let Me In, Book 4 - Cal's POV)

Standalone Novels

Until Valerie: Happily Ever Alpha World

Love At The Bluebird

(co-written with Aurora Rose Reynolds)

Shopping For Love

Bear Creek Rodeo

The Irish Cowboy

The Celtic Cowboy

Acknowledgments

Hi Friends! Hard to believe that this is the end to the Let Me In series… or is it? (insert evil laughter).

In all seriousness, I truly hope you feel I did all of these characters justice, especially Sean, since this was an emotional rollercoaster ride of a story for him.

Just because this may be the end of the series, doesn't mean you won't see your favorite Let Me In series characters in future series. Cal and Jenna have made an appearance in Shopping For Love and I have them scheduled in more books in the future.

I want to thank you, the readers, and the bloggers, for your positive feedback, love and support. Especially to the bloggers, who work long hours to help advertise and support us authors.

Thank you to my family and friends, especially my husband and children. Without their support, I wouldn't be able to continue living my dream.

Thank you to the team of people who helped make Edge of Desire happen.

Thank you to my Misfits for your continued support and promotion of my books!

Please make sure you follow me on all of my social media pages and sign up for my newsletter at authorjessicamarin.com to be up to date with upcoming releases and book signings.

Peace and love,
Jessica

About the Author

Jessica Marin began her love affair with books at a young age from the encouragement of her Grandma Shirley. She has always dreamt of being an author and finally made her dreams of writing happily ever after stories a reality. She currently resides in Tennessee with her husband, children and fur babies.

Jessica would love for you to join her on all of her available social media outlets. Do you love being a part of exclusive reading groups? Then join Jessica Marin's Misfits on Facebook!